A FARAWAY LOOK HAD COME INTO CHAMBRUN'S EYES

He had been holding the black negligee close to his face. He held it away from him now. "Nobody ever wore this thing," he said. "No perfume. No body scent." He bent down and picked up the other items, including the black satin slippers. He turned the slippers over so we could see the soles. "Never worn. Not a scratch on them." He looked at Johnny. "The lady may have intended to wear these things for your father, but she never got around to it."

"Just dropped them and ran when something happened," Jerry said.

"But what happened?" Johnny asked.

"I rather think that's *my* ball game," Chambrun answered.

———————— ★ ————————

HUGH PENTECOST

Bargain with Death

WORLDWIDE.

TORONTO • NEW YORK • LONDON • PARIS
AMSTERDAM • STOCKHOLM • HAMBURG
ATHENS • MILAN • TOKYO • SYDNEY

BARGAIN WITH DEATH

A Worldwide Mystery/April 1989

First published by Dodd, Mead & Company, Inc.

ISBN 0-373-26018-0

PART ONE

ONE

EVERY TIME the little red button blinked on my office telephone, I felt a surge of anger rising in me. There had been no little red button until a month ago. When it blinked, it said, in effect, "Drop anything you're doing, no matter what, and report on the double!" Yes, sir, you sonofabitch—sir!

Like probably a hundred other people who worked at the Hotel Beaumont, my job was a day-to-day thing. It could end tomorrow by edict, or because I couldn't stand it any longer, told Johnny-baby Sassoon what I thought of him, and went somewhere on a six-day drunk. Chambrun had quit a month ago on the day when Johnny-baby suggested that we have topless cigarette girls in the Spartan Bar.

I say Chambrun quit, but that isn't quite accurate. He raised such hell with Papa Sassoon about the whole setup that Joshua Wilfred Sassoon fired him at the cost of about half a million dollars, the balance due on an unexpired ten-year contract. Pierre Chambrun, the Beaumont's legendary manager, was gone but not forgotten. He wasn't very far away, but he could have been in Egypt as far as the hotel's employees were concerned. There are three penthouses on the roof of the Beaumont, known until the arrival of Johnny-baby as the world's top luxury hotel, and two floors of duplex apartments that are cooperatively owned. One

of the penthouses belongs to Chambrun, and while
Joshua Wilfred Sassoon could fire him as manager, he
couldn't remove him from the premises. Penthouse C
was Chambrun's private property, his home, his cas-
tle. He had retired there, he told us, to write his mem-
oirs.

The little red button blinked insistently.

I got up from my desk, slowly, and started along the
corridor to what had been Chambrun's suite of offices. Johnny-baby, damn him, had set himself up in
what had once been the holy-of-holies, Chambrun's
private office.

If you happen to be one of those people who has
read some of the accounts I have written of Pierre
Chambrun's activities, you will know that George
Battle, who called himself the second richest man in
the world and who owned the Beaumont, got himself
into very big trouble and is even now fighting, with all
his resources, to keep himself out of jail for the rest of
his unnatural life. One of his first moves was to liq-
uidate all of his assets, the proceeds, one assumes, to
go into numbered Swiss bank accounts from where
they could be siphoned off to him in some country
from which he couldn't be extradited—if it came to
that. He sold the Beaumont to Joshua Wilfred Sassoon, who was at least the third richest man in the
world, lock, stock and barrel. J. W. Sassoon had no
interest in running a hotel, but he wanted something
to occupy the nonexistent talents of his son Johnny. So
he turned over the magnificent Beaumont to Johnny
as a toy. The topless cigarette girls are an example of
Johnny's notions of "modernizing" the Beaumont.

Chambrun balked and was fired. Most of us on the staff wanted to go with him, but he urged us to stay on and "see what happens." The Beaumont was a living, breathing thing to him; I think he couldn't bear to have her in entirely strange hands.

I walked into the outer office and found myself faced by the mini-skirted tootsie who was Johnny-baby's secretary—at least. She looked strangely as if her makeup had slipped.

"Thank goodness you're here, Mr. Haskell," she said. She waved me to the private office.

I honestly hated to go through the door. The thick Persian rug was gone. The carved Florentine desk was gone. The blue-period Picasso was gone. The sideboard with the Turkish coffee maker was gone. Worst of all, Chambrun was gone.

The idiot boy sat at a very modern chrome-decorated desk, surrounded by framed originals of the center-fold girls from *Playboy* magazine, drinking what had to be a very stiff Scotch-on-the-rocks. It was ten-thirty in the morning.

Johnny-baby is a tall, athletically built young man, with reddish brown hair. He has a kind of round baby face, tanned a beautiful mahogany color. He is, I regret to say, handsome, and he has a wide engaging smile and brown eyes that invite friendship. He looked sick that morning.

"Thank you for coming, Mark," he said.

"It's my job to come when you send for me," I said.

He looked as if I'd hurt him, which pleased me.

"My father is dead," he said.

In my state of mind about the Sassoon family I couldn't feel sorry, but I said I did.

"It appears to have been a heart attack," Johnny-baby said. He took a big swig of his Scotch. "I need your help, Mark."

"With the press?" I asked. I am the public relations man for the Beaumont. Any press releases originate with me.

"Not yet," Johnny-baby said. He lit a cigarette and his hands shook. "The maid found him and reported it to the housekeeper on the ninth floor, a Mrs. Kniffin. Mrs. Kniffin called me and I went right up there."

J. W. Sassoon had taken two adjoining suites on the ninth floor. He was staying with us while Johnny-baby cut his teeth on the Beaumont.

"My father was lying on his bed," Johnny-baby said. "He—he was not wearing anything."

I thought that must have been a sight. The old man had weighed about two hundred and eighty pounds of pure blubber.

"My father always slept in the raw," Johnny-baby said. "I mean, there was nothing odd about his being nude. But—but the bed was all rumpled up, and—Mark, can I tell you something in confidence?"

"Look, Johnny, did you have some doubt about how your father died?" He was my boss, but I was damned if I'd call him Mr. Sassoon.

"Oh, he had a chronic heart condition. I don't think there can be any doubt. The thing that bothers me—well, here it is. On the floor beside the bed was a black lace brassiere, a pair of black lace panties, a pair of black satin bedroom slippers, and a black lace negligee.''

What a way to go, I thought.

"So your father passed out, the lady panicked, and she—'' I looked at him. "Ran out of the suite stark naked?''

"There wasn't any other sign of a woman being there, except a cigarette stub in the bedside ash tray,'' Johnny-baby said. "Lipstick.''

I had an irreverent picture of old J. W. Sassoon and an elaborate call girl. Oh, you can find call girls even in a posh place like the Beaumont. She slips into "something comfortable'' and then slips out. But leave her calling card behind in the form of the black regalia?

"You want me to cover up this aspect of the story for you if I can?'' I asked Johnny-baby. "Or have you already spirited away the lady's undies?''

His eyes looked a little glassy. "It was too late for that,'' he said. "The maid and Mrs. Kniffin had both seen them.''

"Didn't it occur to you they might have a price?'' I asked him, feeling contemptuous. Johnny-baby must have been raised on the theory that every man has his price.

Johnny shook his head. "I don't think so,'' he said.

"Why?'' I asked, mildly surprised. "What makes them different?''

He looked straight at me and there was pain in his brown eyes. "I don't think they like me,'' he said. "Nobody around here likes me, though God knows

I've tried. Would you take a bribe to do something for me, Mark?''

I could have gotten smart-assed and asked him how big a bribe. Instead I just said, ''No.''

Johnny-baby looked down at the empty drink in front of him. ''So I can only ask for your help and hope,'' he said.

''Have you notified the police?'' I asked him.

''Not yet.''

''For Christ sake, man!''

''I had to figure out what to do. That's why I need your help, Mark.''

''Look,'' I said, impatient. ''Your father dies in bed with a hooker. The medical examiner will determine that he had a heart condition and died of it. But you have to go through that routine.''

''It may not have been a heart attack.''

''But you said—''

''I know what I said, Mark.'' He twisted in his chair. ''But it may not have been.''

''Did you even have the house doctor see him?''

''Not yet.'' He turned his head from side to side.

''What are you, a doctor yourself or something? Are you even sure he's dead?''

''No doubt of that,'' Johnny-baby said. ''I was in Vietnam for two years. I know a dead man when I see one.''

''Well, that's something. So let's get Doc Partridge up to Suite 912 and send for the cops.''

''No.''

I shrugged. ''So I don't know any other advice or help to give you, man.''

He looked up at me, quite steady now. "You think I'm a jerk," he said, "and you think my father was a jerk. We've stupidly turned your world upside-down. I was sitting here this morning, just before Mrs. Kniffin called me, wondering if I crawled on my knees to Mr. Chambrun and kissed his foot if he would come back and run the hotel again."

Well, I thought. Well!

"I was an ignorant, presumptuous bastard to think I could do it. My father didn't care whether I could or not. I wanted it, so he gave it to me. Now everybody is laughing at me and hating me at the same time. I deserve it."

It was the damndest thing. Suddenly I liked him. "Look, Johnny, you've got trouble and there are certain routines you have to go through. I'll handle them for you if you say so. I can't answer for Chambrun, but I think he'd agree if he thinks you mean it."

"I'd offer him a new ten-year contract," Johnny said. "But first—"

Strings, I thought. Chambrun wouldn't go for any strings.

"First you have to understand what my trouble is, Mark. I knew my father inside-out, his quirks, his idiosyncrasies. He never had a call girl in his room; never in this world."

"How can you be sure?"

"Because I know him—knew him." He voice broke slightly. "He could throw his weight around in corporations and governments. He could buy power. He could do incredible things like spend millions of dollars to buy me a toy, like the Beaumont. He could afford that. But there were certain rules he lived by. When it came to women and sex, he was a rigid puritan. It would have disgusted him to be involved with a professional whore.''

"So he decided to try it once before it was too late," I said.

"Never! Absolutely not."

"So what do you think happened?"

"Somebody tried to frame him," Johnny-baby said. "Maybe he got so angry it brought on an attack. Maybe he tried, physically, to protect himself."

"What good would it do them to frame him after he was dead?" I asked.

"I don't know. That's what I want to find out before the police come into the picture and draw easy conclusions about it. I thought maybe Mr. Chambrun would have a look at things before we brought in the law. I know he has a reputation for handling difficult situations here in the hotel. Would you tell him I want him back—for keeps? Would you tell him I need his help, need it desperately?"

"I think maybe you're going to have to tell him that yourself," I said.

Johnny Sassoon shook his head. "I'm going to stay with my father," he said. "I've left him alone too long."

PIERRE CHAMBRUN IS A SHORT, dark, square little man with black eyes buried in deep pouches that can be compassionate, twinkle with humor, or turn as cold as a hanging judge's. For years the Beaumont has been his kingdom, a small city within the walls of one building, with its own shops, restaurants, bars, luxury boutiques, hospital units, safety deposit vaults, ballrooms, convention quarters, police force. The staff is Chambrun-trained, Chambrun-efficient. Some people think he has some sort of private radar system, magic eyes in the back of his head. He knows exactly what is going on in his world at every moment of the day and night. It isn't really magic. His people are trained to report to him on the instant anything even slightly out of the usual is happening anywhere in the Beaumont. An incredible loyalty makes it all work with Swiss watch efficiency.

When I got to Penthouse C that morning, Chambrun already knew that J. W. Sassoon was dead. I suspected Mrs. Kniffin had been his eyes and ears.

Miss Ruysdale, Chambrun's incomparable secretary, met me at the front door.

She smiled at me. "Mr. Chambrun is waiting for you," she said. Betsy Ruysdale is a handsome, beautifully turned out woman in her mid-thirties. Normally she presides in the office where Johnny-baby had his mini-skirted tootsie. She protects Chambrun from unnecessary irritations, appears to be able to read his mind, and there is a persistent rumor that she may take care of much more personal needs. He calls her Ruysdale, never Betsy or Miss Ruysdale. Only once, when she was in danger, have I seen him be anything but impersonal about her. Yet we on the staff wondered about them.

"J. W. Sassoon is dead," I told her.

"He knows, Mark."

Of course he would, I thought. I found him in the little paneled study off his living room. The inevitable cup of Turkish coffee, an incredibly vile brew, was by his hand and he was smoking one of his flat Egyptian cigarettes.

"Took you long enough," he said.

"Johnny-baby had me in his office," I said.

"I know."

"Do you also know that he wants you back, will give you a new ten-year contract, and needs your help?" I said, expecting some sign of surprise. I was disappointed.

"It took him longer than I expected," Chambrun said. "What kind of help?"

I told him. He stood up, trying, I thought, not to show too much eagerness at the prospect of getting back into the saddle. He walked out to where Miss Ruysdale stood, still smiling.

"Have Eric bring over the new contract for Sassoon to sign," he said.

"It's already here, Mr. Chambrun."

Chambrun looked at me, his eyes dancing in their pouches. "Let's get down to 912," he said.

As always he had been way ahead of the game.

WHEN WE REACHED the ninth floor, we found Jerry Dodd, the Beaumont's chief security officer, waiting outside 912. Jerry is a shrewd, dark, wiry little man who is, I suspect, next to Miss Ruysdale, Chambrun's most trusted aide. I like to think I rate Number Three.

"Young Sassoon's in there with the body," Jerry said. "He hasn't called the police or had Doc Partridge up to look. He's about as flaky as they come."

"Not so flaky," Chambrun said, smiling. "It may interest you to know that I'm back on the job."

"Hallelujah!" Jerry said.

Chambrun rang the bell and a moment or two later Johnny opened the door for us. He led us back into the living room of 912.

"I'm grateful to you for coming, Mr. Chambrun," he said. "Did Mark tell you—?"

"The new contract is waiting for you to sign when we're through here," Chambrun said. It was so very cold and abrupt that even Chambrun felt it. "We can talk about it, Johnny. I'm glad to help."

We went into the bedroom where the huge body of J. W. Sassoon lay on the king-sized double bed, somehow grotesque in its nakedness. I saw the missing lady's working clothes lying on the floor.

Chambrun moved in a slow circle around the bed, like an animal suspicious of some sort of hidden trap. I found myself staring at the dead man's jowly face. He had died with that face contorted by pain or anger, it was hard to tell which.

Jerry Dodd had picked up the telephone by the bed, covering it first with his handkerchief. I heard him ask for Mrs. Veach, our daytime switchboard supervisor. He wanted a list of out-calls from the suite. He turned to us while he waited.

"If he arranged to have some hooker come to his room, he may have phoned for her from here," Jerry said.

Johnny-baby, looking stricken, shook his head. "He never sent for a girl. He never dreamed of having a girl. I would swear to that."

Jerry gave him a patient grin. "She was here," he said.

Mrs. Veach evidently came back on with a couple of numbers for Jerry. She obviously went on talking after the two numbers she gave him were written down. Jerry listened, frowning. He thanked her and put down the phone.

"Mrs. Veach thinks this instrument is bugged," he said. "They've noticed some kind of interference on it for the last few days."

"Why didn't she report it?" Chambrun asked, his voice sharp.

Jerry glanced at the miserable Johnny-baby. The glance asked why she should have reported it and who she should have reported it to? What went on with the Sassoons was the Sassoons' business.

"Check it," Chambrun said.

Jerry began unscrewing the mouthpiece of the phone. I saw Chambrun pick up the missing lady's negligee.

Jerry gave with a low whistle. He had the phone apart. "Bugged all right," he said. Chambrun came over to look. "Sophisticated little gadget."

"Tiny radio transmitter," Chambrun said.

"It would pick up whatever was said on the phone," Jerry said, "and anything else that was said in this room. Someone somewhere else in the hotel, or anywhere within a block of here, could listen."

"Why?" Johnny Sassoon asked. It was like a cry of pain.

Jerry shrugged. "Your ball game," he said.

A faraway look had come into Chambrun's eyes. He had been holding the black negligee close to his face. He held it away from him now. "Nobody ever wore this thing," he said. "No perfume. No body scent." He bent down and picked up the other items, including the black satin slippers. He turned the slippers over so we could see the soles. "Never worn. Not a scratch on them." He looked at Johnny. "The lady may have intended to wear these things for your father, but she never got around to it."

"Just dropped them and ran when something happened," Jerry said.

"But what happened?" Johnny asked.

"I rather think that's *my* ball game," Chambrun said.

TWO

ELDERLY GENTLEMEN have died of heart failure in the wrong rooms with the wrong companions many times before J. W. Sassoon breathed his last. As I have said, the Beaumont is like a small city. It has its incidence of crime, of sudden death from natural causes, of suicides, and even murder. I suppose, percentage-wise, we have more suicides than the average. Lonely, desperate people come to the plush Beaumont, buy themselves a gourmet dinner, drink our fabulous wines, enjoy our nightclubs in one last splurge, often with their last dollars, and then they hang themselves from a shower rod or swallow a bottle of pills. The natural-unnatural deaths of older men is probably higher than the general average. You have to be rich to spend a day at the Beaumont. Older men are more apt to be that kind of rich and hungry for some last in-dulgence of the flesh. A young secretary, a greedy young mistress, also has a room nearby and the older man goes there and dies of overexercise. What often follows is cover-up—a popular word in Washington these days.

What advantage could there be in insisting that the dead man's indiscretion be made public? It could hurt a wife, a family, and do no one any good. More often that not Chambrun has acted to protect the innocent in such cases. He would probably have acted, unhesitatingly, to cover-up J. W. Sassoon's last indiscretion on earth except for the tiny little transistor placed in the telephone in Sassoon's bedroom. I don't suppose Chambrun gave a damn about what went on in J. W. Sassoon's business or personal life, but he could be a tiger when someone interfered with the Beaumont's routines. Any hotel guest was guaranteed privacy and security from outside intrusions. The Beaumont is located only a few blocks from the United Nations Building on the east side of town and dozens of foreign diplomats made the hotel their home away from home. If phones could be bugged, the promise of privacy and security broke down. Before Chambrun did any covering-up for J. W. Sassoon, he meant to find out who had bugged the telephone and who had left a lady's unworn black lace underthings to compromise the old man's dying.

I have to admit that I didn't really give a hoot about the Sassoons and their problems. I spent the next hour or so after we left 912 emulating Paul Revere, "Chambrun is back!" The gloomy climate which had engulfed the hotel for the last month evaporated like a morning mist. I ran into Mr. Novotny, who is the maitre d' in the Spartan Bar, and he was literally weeping with joy. The nightmare prospect of topless cigarette girls was banished forever.

Chambrun may have been on the trail of an electronics expert, but in the process he had performed another kind of miracle. When I went up to the second floor about two hours after I'd started my Paul Revere routine, I found things changed. Johnny-baby's mini-skirted tootsie was gone, replaced by Miss

Ruysdale in her simple little four-hundred-dollar black dress, smiling her Cheshire cat smile. She gestured toward the holy-of-holies and I went in. The Persian rug was back on the floor, the blue-period Picasso on the wall facing the re-emerged Florentine desk. The Turkish coffee maker was gurgling on the sideboard, and Chambrun sat behind the desk, his black eyes hooded, watching the smoke curl upward from one of his flat Egyptian cigarettes. In the twinkling of an eye God was back in his heaven and all was right with the world.

Standing over by the window was Johnny-baby, looking as though he was waiting for the trash collector to come back for the last memento of a bad dream.

"I take it you have been notifying the staff that I am back here," Chambrun said.

"Yes, sir."

"So, it's time to start running a hotel," Chambrun said. "You will issue a release to the effect that J. W. Sassoon died of a heart attack in the night. No details. Understood?"

"Understood."

"If there is any rumor of a bugged telephone, I'll know that it came from you."

"Or you, or Jerry, or Johnny-baby," I said.

"Don't let your high spirits lead you to impertinence, Mark."

"Sorry."

"Jerry and I will obviously protect the story," Chambrun said. "Mr. Sassoon has his own reasons for keeping it quiet."

Johnny-baby, in defeat, had become "Mr. Sassoon." He turned from the window, his round face haggard.

"You are both unhappily aware that I didn't have what it takes to run a hotel," he said. "I admit it freely. Now a huge financial empire has been dropped in my lap, and I am even less well equipped to deal with it." A little nerve twitched on his cheek. "My father always planned to give me a crash course on the Sassoon empire, but he never got around to it. I don't suppose, even with his heart condition, that he really believed he could ever die. When I walk out of here, I'll be surrounded by business associates, and lawyers, and competitors, and enemies. And, God help me, I don't know which end is up!"

"It could not have been a friend who arranged to have his phone bugged," Chambrun said. "Popular as electronic surveillance has become in business and in government, it isn't used against a man by his friends."

"But who were his enemies?" It was like a cry of pain.

Whoever Johnny-baby's enemies were, we suddenly got a view of his friends. The office door opened and Miss Ruysdale stood there, giving Chambrun a little helpless shrug. A small tornado swept past her. It was a female tornado. At first I thought she was a twelve-year-old child. Long blonde hair swept out behind her like Alice in Wonderland in flight. Her face was plain, without makeup, ornamented by gold-rimmed granny glasses. She had on open-toed sandals and a simple, summer print dress that revealed rather nice thighs and knees. As I've said, there was no makeup on her face, but her toenails were painted a bright scarlet. I don't think she was over five feet tall. She had to reach up on tiptoe to get her arms around Johnny-baby's neck and pull his head down so she could kiss him smack on the mouth.

"Sweetie pie!" she said, just before she made contact. Then, breathless: "How awful for you, pet."

"Miss Woodson—Mr. Chambrun, Mr. Haskell," Johnny-baby said. He touched his lips as if they'd been bruised.

"I'm Trudy Woodson," the girl said, as though we should know there were other Woodsons. She focused on Chambrun. "So you finally had your way!" She looked around the elegant office. "I liked it better the way you had it, sweetie." This to Johnny-baby.

I'd had time now to notice that the simple summer print probably covered a body that belonged in Johnny-baby's collection of center-fold girls from *Playboy*.

"I've brought Mr. Carlson, sweetie," Trudy told Johnny-baby.

We looked toward the door and saw a rather handsome man in his fifties standing next to Miss Ruysdale. Dark curly hair was graying at the temples—the man-of-distinction touch. The crow's-feet at the corners of level gray eyes indicated this was a man not unaccustomed to laughter. He had a wide, generous mouth, and his tall, lean body suggested a regular program of exercise.

"Mr. Raymond Carlson is my father's lawyer," Johnny-baby said.

" 'Counsel' is the fancy word," Carlson said, smiling. Then he turned grave. "I'm most desperately sorry about things, Johnny," he said. "Rest assured I don't believe the story about a woman in your father's room."

"Why not?" Chambrun asked sharply.

"Out of character," Carlson said. "Is it true his telephone was being monitored?"

Chambrun's face had turned rock-hard. Someone had leaked what was meant to be a secret. "How did you hear about it, Mr. Carlson?" he asked.

"One of my assistants brought me the news," Carlson said. "Trudy happened to be in my office and we came as quickly as we could."

"Assistant?"

"A young lawyer on my staff," Carlson said.

"Where did he get the information?"

Carlson shrugged. "I didn't stop to ask him."

Chambrun glanced at Miss Ruysdale. "Get Jerry Dodd up here on the double," he said. He crushed out his cigarette and then took a fresh one from his silver case. He seemed to have lost interest in Carlson. He was staring down at the four telephone instruments on his desk.

"I suppose all hell has broken loose in father's office," Johnny-baby said.

Carlson nodded. "The stock market is already doing some surprising things." His smile was wry. "There are a lot of decisions you're going to have to make, Johnny. You're aware that the whole situation is now in your hands?"

"What situation?" Johnny-baby said. "Jesus, Ray, you know I don't know which end is up."

"We'll give you plenty of help, boy."

"He doesn't need help!" Trudy announced. She had planted herself in front of Johnny-baby, her gold head not coming up to his chin, her legs spread apart, hands on her hips. "It's time you ran your own life, Johnny. It's time you grew up!"

"Oh, God!" he said.

Well, anyway, he had five feet of towering support, I thought.

"What arrangements have you made for your father?" Carlson asked.

"Arrangements?" Johnny-baby sounded as if he'd been asked to explain the Einstein theory.

"The police are in charge at the moment," Chambrun said. "It's routine. The Medical Examiner's office has to determine cause of death—just in case."

"No doubt about its being his heart," Carlson said. "He's had three attacks of varying severity. Dr. Millhouse has warned him there could be another one at any moment. Any sudden excitement, overexertion—" Carlson shrugged. "If he discovered his phone was bugged, or someone tried to pull the old badger game on him, he could have gone like—that!"

"Badger game?" Johnny-baby asked.

"Some woman trying to frame him on a morals charge," Carlson said.

"But that's absurd," Johnny-baby said.

"Not in the public prints," Carlson said. "People might believe—"

Chambrun lifted his heavy eyelids. "I take it criminal law isn't your specialty, Mr. Carlson."

"Lord, no," Carlson said. "Corporation stuff is my thing."

"Then you wouldn't have an opinion about how often a perfect murder is committed?"

"Is there such a thing as a perfect murder?" Carlson asked, not very interested, I thought.

"We'll see," Chambrun said.

At that point Jerry Dodd appeared—on the double.

"This place is bugged," Chambrun said, gesturing toward the four telephone instruments.

Without a word Jerry went to work on the phone. We all watched, fascinated. He took each instrument apart, one after the other, and put them together again.

"Clean," he said finally.

"The place is still bugged," Chambrun said.

Jerry began to go over the room. He looked behind the pictures, under the edges of Chambrun's desk and the sideboard. In the corner of the room he stopped, knelt down by the baseboard.

"Jackpot," he said.

It looked like the same little transistor device we'd found in J. W. Sassoon's phone. Jerry examined it closely. "It's been there for quite a while," he said. "Covered by the edge of the rug."

"But this rug just went down!" Johnny-baby said.

"You had a rug of your own down there, didn't you?" Chambrun asked.

"Yes, but—"

"Someone on the listening end knew enough to call your assistant, Mr. Carlson. Bugging phones or installing other kinds of listening devices is a corporate specialty these days, isn't it? It's called, politely, industrial espionage."

"But why Johnny's office?" Carlson asked.

"You tell me."

"It doesn't make sense."

"But there was a pipeline to your office, Carlson. Your assistant knew things that were being very carefully kept secret here."

"So we'll ask him how he knew," Carlson said.

"I urge it," Chambrun said. "By the way, who benefits from J. W. Sassoon's death beside his son and heir?"

"Oh, Lord, big business interests, competitors. Why do you ask?"

"A listening device in a man's bedroom, another in his son's office, don't suggest fun and games," Chambrun said. "Did your father use this office, Johnny?"

"I don't think he came in here twice," Johnny said.

"You weren't involved in his business affairs at all?"

"Lord, no, sir."

Chambrun's eyes were narrowed. "There may be other electric ears around the place, Jerry," he said. "Your job is to find out."

"Right."

Chambrun turned to Carlson. "I'd like to talk to your associate, Mr. Carlson, who told you there'd been a woman in Sassoon's room. If someone in the hotel leaked that news, there's going to be a lynching."

THE FORMAL ANNOUNCEMENT of J. W. Sassoon's death, it was decided, would be made by Raymond Carlson, his lawyer. It was important, Carlson thought, for Johnny-baby to go down to Wall Street to the dead man's offices. There would be a flood of questions coming in which, officially, only the new head of the empire could answer. Johnny, in a sweat of panic at the prospect, was assured by the amiable Mr. Carlson that the right answers would be provided for him.

The small blonde tornado held out an imperious hand to her young man. "The key to your room, Johnny," she said. "I'll wait for you there."

He gave her the key and he and Carlson took off.

I went down the hall to my office. I would have to prepare a statement for the hotel. We'd be swamped with news people when the story broke.

The girl in my outer office told me there was someone waiting to see me. She'd written down the name.

"Mr. A. Gamayel," she said.

"I can't see him now."

"He said he would wait until you could see him." She giggled. "He said it was a matter of life and death."

For a moment I couldn't think who Mr. A. Gamayel was. Then my mental card index file of names relating to the hotel flipped over. Mr. A. Gamayel was part of the United Nations list of diplomats and officials. I recalled a small, dark, lithe little man, olive-skinned, with a toothpaste ad smile and shiny black eyes. I couldn't remember which of the Arab countries he came from at that moment.

Gamayel was standing by my office windows, looking out toward the East River. My office smelled as if I'd had a woman visitor who wore a musky perfume. Gamayel spun around from the window when I closed the office door as though he expected to be attacked. He was youngish, not more than thirty, I thought. He was wearing a black silk suit and a flamboyant yellow tie.

"Oh, it's you, Mr. Haskell," he said. His voice was soft, almost musical.

"I'm sorry I don't have time for you at the moment," I said. "There's an emergency I have to handle."

"Sassoon?" he asked.

The word was evidently out.

"My problem is simple," Gamayel said. "I must get into Sassoon's room. I went up to 912 as soon as I heard, but the police were in charge and they wouldn't let me in."

He took a yellow silk handkerchief out of his breast pocket and touched it to his forehead. In spite of my air-conditioning there was a fine film of sweat there.

"There's no way I can let you into the room," I said.

"You must!" he said. "Let me explain. Last night after dinner I gave Sassoon some documents to look at. They are very secret documents, Mr. Haskell. How do you call them—top secret, classified? If they get into the wrong hands or are made public, God help us all."

"I still can't get you into the room if the police say no," I said. "Whatever Sassoon had in his possession will probably be turned over to his lawyer or his son."

"Impossible!" Gamayel said.

"I don't know what I can do for you, Mr. Gamayel."

"You have heard of something called the energy crisis?" Gamayel asked. "Gas and crude oil shortages?"

"Yes."

"My part of the world holds the answers in the palms of its hands, so to speak." Gamayel refolded the yellow handkerchief and replaced it in his breast pocket. "The great powers are all trying to deal with us, or to be more exact, trying to force us to deal with them. Sassoon was the head man of one of the biggest oil conglomerates in the Western world. I—I was authorized to make him a secret offer. The outlines of that offer were in the documents I gave him to study. If they are made public, my government may well be overthrown and the Communist world come into possession of oil supplies that your world can't do without, Mr. Haskell. I must retrieve those documents."

It sounded like Sherlock Holmes or James Bond, but Gamayel was so intense I halfway believed his melodrama.

"It would be an act of patriotism if you would help me get into that room," Gamayel said.

"There's only one person who might be able to help you," I said. "If you can convince Mr. Chambrun."

"I thought he was no longer connected with the hotel."

"He is back in charge," I said.

Gamayel flashed his bright smile. He seemed to grow younger. "How marvelous," he said. "He was once a great friend of my father's. He will understand the urgency of this situation."

"So let's go ask him," I said.

We set off down the hall together. He was bouncy with enthusiasm. I found the perfume almost overpowering. Miss Ruysdale, looking oddly tense, was in her office. I told her Mr. Gamayel needed to see the boss.

"Perhaps you should go in and ask him," she said. I saw by her manner that something unusual was up. Gamayel reluctantly took a chair she offered him and I went into the inner sanctum.

Chambrun wasn't alone. With him was an old friend of the hotel's, Lieutenant Hardy of the Manhattan Homicide Squad. Hardy is a big, blond man who looks like a slightly thick-headed professional football player rather than the extremely shrewd investigator he is. He was sitting in a chair beside Chambrun's desk, fumbling with a charred black briar pipe. Chambrun looked at me from under his heavy lids.

"Hardy isn't here to pay a social call," he said.

"Sassoon?" I asked.

"The Medical Examiner found pieces of lint in Sassoon's nasal passages and his bronchial tubes,"

Hardy said. "We think he was smothered with a pillow."

"Not a heart attack?"

"Possibly—brought on by his struggle with someone who was trying to kill him," Hardy said. He blew through the stem of his pipe and seemed disappointed with the result. He put the pipe in his pocket. "So far nothing to go on."

I thought about Gamayel and his top-secret documents. I didn't blurt it out to Hardy. I wanted to talk to Chambrun first, just in case Gamayel had told me something like the truth.

Hardy sighed. "A man with a thousand enemies," he said. "Not just people, but governments and combines and God knows what else. Hard to know where to start."

"You start with his lawyer, his son, his business associates," Chambrun said. "He was covered by those damned listening devices. Someone was very close by, watching him, listening to him. He must have been involved in some kind of big deal that someone was trying to mess up for him."

I couldn't hold it in. "There's someone in the outer office who may know something about it," I said. I told them about Mr. Gamayel and his needs. I saw Chambrun press the button on his desk and Miss Ruysdale appeared and was asked to send in Gamayel. Hardy looked almost cheerful.

Gamayel was all smiles for a moment. Then I told him.

"They think Sassoon was murdered," I said. I introduced Hardy. "I'm sorry, but I had to tell them about you."

I thought Gamayel was going to burst into tears. "Someone's got them," he said. "Someone's taken my documents. They killed him when he tried to stop them!"

"Let's go see," Hardy said.

We went out to the bank of elevators on the second floor. While we waited for a car, Hardy turned his blue eyes on the little Arab diplomat. "You understand, Mr. Gamayel, if we find your papers, we won't be able to turn them over to you."

I thought Gamayel's eyes were going to pop out of his head. "But they belong to me! No one else must see them."

"Everything in Sassoon's room will remain in police custody until we're sure there isn't a lead there, and until we know for certain to whom they belong."

"But they belong to me—the documents," Gamayel said.

Hardy smiled at him. "If we simply take your word for that, Mr. Gamayel, we might be turning over those papers to someone who isn't entitled to them. Claiming them isn't proof of the right to take possession."

Gamayel looked stunned.

The elevator door opened and the operator gave Chambrun a broad grin. "Nice to have you back, Mr. Chambrun," the boy said.

"Thank you, Emil." Chambrun knew the first name of every one of several hundred employees in the hotel.

We were whisked up to the ninth floor. One of Hardy's men was stationed outside the door of 912. "Sergeant Kramer's still inside, Lieutenant," the man said.

Kramer, owlish behind shell-rimmed glasses, looked more like a college professor than a cop. He glanced at a notebook he was holding. "Half a dozen sets of prints, Lieutenant," he said. "The maid, the house-keeper, Sassoon himself. Three other sets we haven't identified, one set on the woman's clothing and the lipstick-stained cigarette butt. Another on the head-board of the bed, high up, as if a man had braced himself there. A third all over the desk here in the sit-ting room."

Gamayel was staring at the desk, which looked as if it had never been used, just as it might have been when a guest first checked in.

"The maid remembers that the desk had been loaded with papers and a briefcase," Kramer said. "She remembers because Sassoon had told her not to touch anything there if she didn't want to be fired."

"No papers or briefcase anywhere else?" Hardy asked.

Kramer shook his head. Gamayel groaned.

"Looks like the killer cleaned him out," Hardy said.

Chambrun had walked across to the door of the bedroom and was looking in. I gathered the body was no longer there. He turned his head.

"It's just possible Johnny took his father's things," he said. "He doesn't seem to have understood just

how he should behave in the situation. See if you can
reach him at Raymond Carlson's office, Mark."

I asked Kramer if it was all right to use the phone
there. He said it was okay, they'd been over it. Mrs.
Veach looked up the number for me and put me
through. I had some trouble with a protective secretary getting through to Carlson, but I finally made it.

"Johnny started back to the hotel a few minutes
ago, Mr. Haskell," Carlson said. "By the way, would
you give a message to Mr. Chambrun for me?"

"Of course."

"My associate here in the office, Donald Webster,
tells me he got the news of J.W.'s death and the details from a man named Mark Zorich who works for
J.W. and who's registered there at the Beaumont. Don
didn't have any reason to ask Zorich how he knew. No
reason why he should."

"Thanks. I'll pass it on," I said, and I did.

"I think we better talk with Mr. Zorich," Chambrun said.

I called Mrs. Veach on the switchboard again and
asked for Zorich's room number. Such an inquiry is
usually a matter of seconds. Mrs. Veach took longer
on this and finally came back with the word that she
had no record of anyone named Zorich being registered. I checked with Mr. Atterbury at the front desk.
No one named Zorich was registered or had been registered according to his records.

Chambrun looked irritated. Under his management daily registration cards were delivered to him.
Hotel guests might have been surprised or even outraged if they could have seen those cards. In addition

to a name and address, there were code markings on them. If a guest was an alcoholic, it showed there. If he was a woman chaser, a husband cheating on his wife or a wife cheating on her husband, it showed. Credit ratings showed. If there was any other special knowledge about the guest, like his business, his diplomatic connections if he had any, his personal connections with anyone we knew, it showed. Chambrun hadn't seen any of those cards for a month. He had no way, at that moment, of knowing whether the system had been continued under Johnny-baby's eccentric management.

"Ask Atterbury to check and provide me with a list of everyone who had reservations made for them by J. W. Sassoon or Johnny," Chambrun said.

I called Atterbury back and relayed the message. I noticed while I talked that Gamayel was jittering around like Mr. Coffee-Nerves. He kept blotting at his face with that yellow silk handkerchief.

"I protest your right to take possession of my documents, Lieutenant," he said, "but I'd be a great deal happier to know that they were in your hands than someone else's. Since young Mr. Sassoon isn't here, would it be possible to look in his rooms, just to make sure?"

"He started up from Wall Street a few minutes ago," Chambrun said. "It shouldn't take him too long."

I was already late in preparing a statement for the news people and I went back down to my office. Two or three reporters were already clamoring. It was, of course, a big story. J. W. Sassoon was a world figure.

We weren't telling it all; nothing about the black lace frills, nothing about the certainty that Sassoon's death, while it may technically have been a heart attack, was in Hardy's opinion a murder. Everyone wanted to talk to Johnny-baby. The King was dead, long live the King.

I guess that first assault on me must have lasted nearly an hour. Sooner or later the news boys would get to Johnny-baby, like it or not. I had a feeling he ought to be briefed by Chambrun and Hardy before he came out on center stage. I kept calling his room, but got no answer. I alerted Johnny Thacker, the day bell captain, to have Johnny call me the minute he showed up in the lobby. Miss Ruysdale assured me he hadn't turned up at the boss's office. I had a picture of him sitting in the park and feeding the pigeons while he tried to pull himself together. Finally I headed for Chambrun's office to express my concern that the news boys might get to him before we could tell him what to say.

Mr. Gamayel was still with Chambrun, still sweating and blotting with his yellow handkerchief. Hardy had gone somewhere. Chambrun looked dark as a thundercloud. Before I could say anything, he handed me three registration cards.

"Reservations made by J. W. Sassoon," he said.

I gave them a quick look. The first was for a James Olin. There was nothing on the card, not even an address, to indicate anything except that Sassoon had asked for a room for him. The second was for a Mrs. Valerie Brent, address London, England, reservation made by Sassoon. The code indicated that she was a widow, not grass, with an A-1 credit rating, who had stayed with us once before some five years ago. The information on her dated back to that time and wasn't necessarily current. The third card was for Emory Clarke, address Boston, Massachusetts. I didn't really have to read the dope sheet on this man. He was a millionaire oil man, his main interests in Central and South America. He had been an adviser to Presidents, served as a special consultant to the State Department during one administration, turned down the ambassadorship to Great Britain. He had stayed at the Beaumont many times in the past and he wouldn't have had to ask J. W. Sassoon to get him a suite. I had talked to him several times and thought of him as a shaggy replica of that late, great actor, Charles Laughton. There was, I noticed, no Mark Zorich.

I was just handing the cards back to Chambrun when Hardy reappeared.

"No sign of young Sassoon?" he asked.

I told him I'd been trying to locate Johnny and had people alerted to let me know the moment he showed.

"I think I'd like to have a look in his room," Hardy said. "If he cleaned off his father's desk and took the stuff to his room, we'll know we aren't looking for a thief as well as a killer." He smiled at Gamayel. "It might also make our friend feel a little easier."

Chambrun picked up his phone and asked Jerry Dodd to meet us on the twelfth floor with a passkey. The four of us went up to twelve and arrived at the same time as Jerry. We knocked on the door, got no answer, and Jerry opened it with his key.

So help me, I had completely forgotten about Miss Trudy Woodson. She was sitting up in Johnny's bed, a sheet pulled around her, quite obviously hiding her delightful nakedness. Her clothes were draped neatly over the back of a chair.

Her eyes were blazing. "What the hell do you creeps mean by barging in here?" she wanted to know.

"We knocked," Hardy said, undisturbed. "No one answered."

"So no one answered, so nobody wanted you in, so get out!"

Hardy showed his police shield. "We're looking for some papers and a briefcase young Sassoon may have brought here from his father's room."

"So ask Johnny when he gets here—if he ever gets here!"

"I'm afraid we'll have to look for them now," Hardy said. "If you'd like to put on some clothes—?"

"I'm quite content the way I am," Trudy said. She sat there, defiant, the sheet pulled up around her chin.

Johnny-baby had just a large single room and bath. He hadn't gone for a suite for himself. Hardy went methodically through the desk, the bureau, the two closets, the bathroom. He came back from that last place and stood looking down at the little blonde time bomb on the bed.

"If you don't mind," he said, "I'd like to look under and in the bed."

"I do mind."

"Then you'll have to forgive me," Hardy said, and reached for the sheet.

She was out of bed in a flash, the sheet clutched around her, screaming unprintable obscenities at him. She had a vocabulary that would have put a long-shoreman to shame. Hardy went methodically about the business of searching and found nothing.

"Thank you, ma'am," he said cheerfully.

"You bastard!" she said, using her least offensive language.

"Looks like your documents aren't here, Mr. Gamayel," Hardy said.

"Sorry to disturb you, Miss Woodson," Chambrun said.

We all started for the door. I was last.

"Haskell!" Trudy called out to me.

I went back into the room.

"You're cute," she said. She was back on the bed. The sheet was now revealing golden shoulders.

"Thanks," I said.

"I'm never really myself," she said, "unless I've had my ration of sex before lunch. Would you care to oblige?"

I just stared at her, my mouth going dry as she slowly lowered the sheet. "Johnny wouldn't like it," I said.

"He knew I was waiting for him," Trudy said. "If he didn't want it, to hell with him."

I stared at what was there to see. "I'm afraid I'm involved in investigating a murder," I said, like an ass.

"So somebody did kill the old poop," she said. Her smile was dazzling. "You may regret this all the rest of your life, Haskell. But just so that you'll know what you've missed, I'll give you a rain check."

Somehow I got out of there and down the hall to join the others by the elevators. Chambrun gave me a wry smile, and I realized I'd joined Mr. Gamayel in the sweat department.

"So you got away," Chambrun said.

I muttered something.

"I don't suppose it will stop you if I tell you that young lady is poison," he said.

"You're just jealous," I managed to say.

THREE

By TWO-THIRTY THAT AFTERNOON Johnny-baby had
still not reappeared at the Beaumont. I was in and out
of Chambrun's office during that gap in time, and I
could sense a kind of tension beginning to mount.
Hardy had been in touch with Chambrun, and there
was no longer any question in the Lieutenant's mind
that someone had tried to smother J. W. Sassoon with
his bed pillow, bringing on a fatal heart attack. Murder-one.

Hardy, in his methodical fashion, had questioned
the floor maid, Mrs. Kniffin, the housekeeper, bell-
hops, elevator operators, Mike Maggio, the night bell
captain, and God knows who else. There had been no
noticed comings and goings from J. W. Sassoon's suite
the night of his death. The list of out-going phone calls
was minimal. Sassoon had called his broker just after
the close of the market that afternoon—a routine daily
call. He had called his office twice, checked out as
routine business calls. Room Service had provided him
with a steak dinner for one, a mixed green salad, and
a bottle of champagne at eight o'clock in the evening.
So far, the Room Service waiter was one of the last
persons to report having seen J. W. Sassoon alive.
Gamayel, delivering his documents, may have been
later. Alive, eager for his dinner, generous with his tip.
But, of course, there had been others, or at least one

other, later. There had been someone who had forced
a pillow down on J. W. Sassoon's face—J. W. Sassoon stark naked—bracing himself against the headboard of the bed. There had been the lady who'd left
her black underwear by the bed. There had been a
third set of prints in the desk.

"Unless the killer left those unworn garments as a
decoy," Chambrun pointed out.

Check, and check, and keep checking is Hardy's
game plan always. There were labels in the black underwear which led the detective to a fashionable Park
Avenue boutique. Brassiere, panties, negligee and
slippers, a complete enough order for a salesgirl to remember. Remember only that the things had been
purchased by a stylish-looking woman, probably
about thirty, who had paid for them with cash. No
charge account, nothing to lead to the buyer. The
salesgirl might just remember her if she saw her again,
only because she had been particularly courteous and
considerate, evidently a rarity.

So much for careful police work. The three sets of
unidentified fingerprints had been forwarded to the
FBI for examination. Hardy guessed one of them
might belong, innocently enough, to Johnny-baby. It
would save some time if Johnny-baby would just show
up. It began to look as though feeding the pigeons in
the park wouldn't hold water.

Chambrun suggested I inquire of Trudy Woodson
if she knew where Johnny-baby could be. I tried on the
phone. No answer. I had Mrs. Kniffin, the housekeeper, send a floor maid to Johnny's room with clean
towels. Trudy had, to use a colloquialism, split.

Chambrun has a way of getting things done, orders obeyed, that another man couldn't. Things must have been even more tangled and tense at the offices of J. W. Sassoon than they were at the Beaumont. A huge segment of wealth and power was about to change hands. The enemy must be out in full cry, trying to rip off a share for themselves. And yet, at Chambrun's request, Raymond Carlson, the dead man's counsel, left what must have been a whirlpool of activity to come to the Beaumont, bringing with him a junior associate named Donald Webster. Webster, an Ivy League type, was the one who had gotten the word from the man named Mark Zorich that J. W. Sassoon was dead and that there had been a woman in the old man's room.

Carlson looked five years older than he had that morning. He was still amiably polite, but harried. He was shocked by the news that we were dealing with a homicide. It added to the complications in his life.

"It means holding up a great many important decisions," he said. "If J.W. was murdered, we have to be sure that nobody gains by it."

We were in Chambrun's office with Hardy.

"A simple-minded question, Mr. Carlson," the Lieutenant said. "Who might gain?"

Carlson shook his head wearily. "It's so complex, Lieutenant, it's almost impossible to answer. There's Johnny, of course. But after that—?" He shrugged his sagging shoulders. "It's like a chess game, with the players thinking half a dozen moves ahead. There are so many irons in the fire, so many possibilities. Only the players know who might gain by the old man's death tomorrow, or next week, or next month. Or even next year. The moves are thought of that far in advance."

"Let's get down to some simple questions," Chambrun said, his eyes buried deep in their pouches. I knew the signs of impatience. "Where is Johnny Sassoon? He left your office over three and a half hours ago, presumably to come back here."

"No idea," Carlson said. "He said he wanted to get back here to stay on top of what was happening. I thought he might be running away from what he had to face at the office, but I had no doubt he was coming back here. He may still be running. You have no idea of the load that's descended on him—a load he isn't even remotely equipped to carry."

"But he has you and other loyal troops," Chambrun said.

"God help us all. J. W. Sassoon had a computer for a mind. The rest of us are just ordinarily bright human beings, but with no buttons to push."

Chambrun turned his attention to the Ivy League. "A man named Mark Zorich called you to tell you that J. W. Sassoon was dead, Mr. Webster?"

"Yes, sir."

"He also told you there was evidence to suggest the old man's heart may have given out in the midst of a sex adventure?"

"Yes, sir. Zorich got the word to us as quickly as he could. He knew how important it was to us."

"Did he tell you how he knew?"

"No, sir."

"It was a pretty complete report—about the lady and all."

"Yes, sir. No details, of course. Just the basic information."

"You know Zorich?"

"Not personally, sir. He's been a telephone contact ever since I went to work for Mr. Carlson."

Carlson nodded. "Mark Zorich has been a sort of private aide to J.W. for the last twenty years. What shall I call him? An undercover investigator? He's relayed messages to me hundreds of times on the telephone, but would you believe I've never laid eyes on him?"

"But he's registered here in the hotel?"

"So he told me," Webster said.

"Well, he isn't," Chambrun said. "At least not under the name of Zorich."

"He didn't say he was registered under the name of Zorich, sir," Webster said. "He just said he was registered here."

"It may sound very cloak-and-dagger," Carlson said, "but I have the feeling Zorich used a number of aliases. The nature of the work he did for J.W."

"So even 'Zorich' may be an alias and his real name is something else?"

"'Zorich' is the name he's used with us for twenty years," Carlson said.

"But neither of you would know him if you saw him?"

"I'm afraid not," Carlson said.

"Do you have a way to reach him? A phone number, a mailbox?" Chambrun asked.

"He contacted us, we never contacted him," Carlson said.

Chambrun reached for the three registration cards on his desk. He handed one to Carlson. "Who is James Olin?"

Carlson frowned. "No idea," he said.

"Sassoon reserved a room for him," Chambrun said. "He's still registered in, but we haven't been able to locate him. Could he be 'Zorich'?"

"I just don't know, Mr. Chambrun. I never heard the name James Olin."

Chambrun handed him a second card. "Mrs. Valerie Brent?"

I saw a nerve twitch high up on Carlson's cheek. "She's here in the hotel?" he asked.

"Suite arranged for by Sassoon," Chambrun said. "I take it you know her."

Carlson nodded slowly. Somehow he was no longer a "man of distinction." His handsome face looked haggard and old. "Yes, I know Valerie," he said. That was all he said.

"That card indicates she's a widow," Chambrun said. "Home base London. Extremely well off financially. What was her connection with Sassoon?"

Carlson drew a deep breath. "You'll find out anyway if you keep digging," he said. "Valerie is an American. Her husband—her late husband—was Michael Brent, a British journalist and author. Free lance. Into very important stories in the world of politics and big business. A couple of years ago he was preparing to do a book on the J. W. Sassoon empire. The old man seemed to like him, gave him access to all

kinds of information that had been more or less secret over the years. The Brents were based in London,
but toward the end of the research period they came
to New York and stayed in a house in the East Sixties
that the old man rented for them. The old man opened
all kinds of doors for Michael Brent. He seemed
pleased that there was going to be some kind of glam-
orized account of his career. And then—"

"Michael Brent was murdered," Hardy said unexpectedly.

Carlson nodded.

Hardy was fingering his black pipe with no apparent purpose. "One I fumbled," he said, his voice
sounding harsh. "One I wanted badly to break and
fumbled." He glanced at Chambrun. "I should have
made the connection. Valerie Brent—Mrs. Michael
Brent. Maybe I wanted to forget." He put his pipe
back in his pocket. "Michael Brent was shot between
the eyes sitting at his desk in his study in that Sixtieth
Street house. The shot killed him. He was also bru-
tally slashed up with a knife, disfigured, mutilated.
Jesus, I wanted that killer."

"How did you miss?" Chambrun asked.

"A dozen dead-end streets," Hardy said. "Reams
of paper had been burned in the fireplace in that study.
A manuscript and a carbon of the manuscript and
stacks of notes and tapes, Mrs. Brent told us. She told
us her husband had been writing a sort of biography
of J. W. Sassoon. An approved biography, you understand. Sassoon was outraged. He had, he told us,
very much wanted that biography finished and published. It had to be enemies of his, perhaps revealed in

an unpleasant light in the book, who had slaughtered Michael Brent. Who? Like in this case, there were hundreds of possibilities.''

Hardy stopped and Carlson looked at him, waiting for him to go on. Chambrun watched.

"There's more," he said.

"Mrs. Brent didn't buy it. She was, naturally, pretty hysterical.''

"She loved Michael," Carlson said.

"Things her husband had said to her before he was killed made her think he'd come up with some dirt on Sassoon," Hardy said. "She thought her husband and Sassoon had quarreled over this. Michael Brent was going to print the dirt whether Sassoon liked it or not. She was convinced Sassoon had ordered Michael Brent destroyed.''

"She hadn't a shred of proof," Carlson said. "I was J.W.'s lawyer, of course. She didn't even know what the 'dirt' was her husband had unearthed. There was absolutely nothing pointing to J.W.—except his interest in Michael, in the book, in the help he had given Michael in preparing it.''

"Dead end," Hardy said. He shook his head. "God how she hated me for not being able to pin it on Sassoon.''

"When the case was closed," Carlson said, "I begged her—''

"The case wasn't closed," Hardy said, angry. "No unsolved murder case is closed.''

Carlson shrugged. "When there was nothing more to be done, J.W. offered her a handsome financial settlement. She refused. She didn't need money and she wouldn't have taken any from him if she had. I remember her passionate intensity the last time I saw her. She was going to nail J.W. if it took her a lifetime."

The room was silent for a moment.

"Yet she's here at the Beaumont," Chambrun said, "in Sassoon's hotel, in a suite arranged for by him— her enemy. How do you account for that, Mr. Carlson?"

"I don't. I can't," Carlson said.

The office door burst open, an unheard-of happening, and Trudy Woodson came charging into the office, a ruffled Miss Ruysdale behind her. Seeing Ruysdale without her cool was an event in itself.

"I'm sorry, Mr. Chambrun," she said. "I had my back turned for a minute—"

Ray Carlson gave Ruysdale a wry smile. "I sympathize, Miss Ruysdale," he said. "Trudy has been known to get by security police in our office."

Trudy faced Chambrun across his desk, hands on her hips, jaw jutting forward. "All right, buster," she said, "what have you done with Johnny?"

"We've been trying to find you to ask you what *you'd* done with him," Chambrun said.

Trudy turned on Carlson. "You've got him shut away down in that damned office of yours!" she said. "Couldn't you even let him call me?"

"He left the office over three hours ago," Carlson said. Trudy seemed to have brought him back to life a little. Webster, the Ivy League character, was quite clearly undressing her in his mind's eye.

"I'll break his back when he shows up," Trudy said. She looked at me. "I'll be waiting in Johnny's room—in case you have any news, Haskell."

She turned on her heel and walked out. Carlson was grinning at me and I think I was blushing. Carlson evidently knew she wasn't interested in news.

Chambrun was all business. "I want James Olin the minute he shows up," he said to me. "I'd like to talk with Mrs. Brent, if it's all right with you, Hardy. And Emory Clarke, if you can find him."

"I want them all, too," Hardy said.

"We're up to our necks in trouble at the office," Carlson said. "Don and I must get back there if you're through with us."

"For now," Chambrun said.

"If this man Zorich gets in touch with you, tell him I want to talk to him," Hardy said.

SO WE HAD A MURDER, and a missing heir, and people to talk to if we could find them. And, Chambrun reminded me, a hotel to run. I was swamped by reporters from the media. So far all I could or would tell them was that J. W. Sassoon had died of a heart attack. If they wanted stuff on the old man, Raymond Carlson was their boy. But we live in a world of leaks, and the word was out that there was something more in the air than a cardiac failure.

"The place is crawling with cops!" I was reminded.

"Routine," I kept saying. "Someone dies unexpectedly, it's routine to check out."

"Why is a Homicide man in charge?"

"You'll have to ask him."

We weren't going to be able to cover up for very long, I saw. Then we'd have newsmen crawling out of the woodwork. It was important to get James Olin and Mrs. Brent and Emory Clarke to Chambrun before they were swarmed under by curious reporters. Olin and Mrs. Brent didn't answer their room phones, but some sort of secretary answered promptly in Clarke's suite. Mr. Clarke was, she told me, at the United Nations in conference with someone or other. She thought she might be able to reach him and tell him Chambrun and Hardy wanted to talk to him.

James Olin had one of the less expensive rooms on the fourth floor of the hotel. "Less expensive" is a relative phrase at the Beaumont—like fifty dollars a day. Neither the maid nor the housekeeper for that floor could tell me much about him. He had been in the hotel for about a week, paid his bill promptly when it was presented, used an American Express credit card for that purpose. The night maid had seen him once when she went to his room to turn down his bed. All she could remember was that he was tall, rather sharp with her in saying he didn't want his bed turned down, and that he wore green-tinted glasses.

I checked out on his American Express card. We have a kind of mutual exchange of credit information with them. James Olin had no home address. They billed him through his bank, the Waltham Trust in Chicago. He'd carried the card for some eight years and his bills were paid promptly. It was too late in the day to get any information from the bank. American

Express told me he had listed his occupation, when he applied for a card, as "investment counselor."

By the time I got through collecting facts on James Olin, I had a call from Johnny Thacker, the day bell captain, that Mrs. Valerie Brent had returned to the hotel and gone up to her room on the eighth floor. But she didn't pick up the phone when I called her.

I went up to the eighth floor and knocked on her door.

"Who is it?" a pleasant, low voice asked.

"It's Mark Haskell, Mrs. Brent. Hotel management."

There was a moment's hesitation and then the door was opened and I saw Valerie Brent for the first time. You can describe a person with words and not come even close to conveying the impact that person has on you.

She had a beautifully made face—high cheek-bones, a strong, molded chin, a generous mouth, wide, very candid hazel eyes. Her hair was a darkish red—natural, I was certain. She had the figure of a high-fashion model—slim, erect, curved where it ought to be, flat where it ought to be—long, elegant tanned legs.

She gave me an unexpected dazzling smile, and that's when my knees began to buckle. I had expected a grieving widow woman, or perhaps a vengeful Medea. This was the handsomest gal I could ever remember seeing, with so much vitality, energy, and sheer electric excitement she took your breath away. Not a professional sex-peddler, you understand; just an unbelievable, outgoing radiance.

"My dear Mark Haskell," she said in her deep, husky voice, "I swear, by all that's holy, I meant to look you up, but I've been so darn tangled up in things— Do come in. Will you forgive me?"

"Almost anything," I said, "except if you were supposed to look me up and didn't."

A tiny little frown creased her forehead. "You are Shelda Mason's Mark Haskell, aren't you?" she asked.

Now Shelda Mason is another story. Shelda is a girl who was once my secretary. She is a girl in whose apartment two blocks from the hotel I kept shaving equipment and a change of clothes. We had a parting and Shelda went to Europe for a year to work for George Battle, who at that time owned the Beaumont. Not too long ago she had come back and we had made it together again. At the present moment she had gone west to visit her parents, whom she hadn't seen for a year. But as I looked at this extraordinary woman, God forgive me, Shelda, I didn't want to be thought of as belonging to anybody. I wanted to be free to put all my chips on the red.

"If Shelda steered you my way, she is both an idiot and a fairy godmother," I said.

Her laugh stirred up butterflies in my stomach. "She said you were a hopelessly charming flirt."

"'Hopeless' isn't a word I like to think of at the moment," I said. "Where did you and Shelda meet?"

"In London, a couple of months ago," Valerie said. "She had come over from the south of France on an errand for George Battle. I met her at a friend's house. I told her I was going to New York, would be staying at the Beaumont. She told me to be sure to look you up, that you were a doll and might be feeling lonely. Didn't she tell you?''

Shelda hadn't told me anything. We'd been too busy in the crisis that destroyed George Battle and in getting together again.

"If she had," I told Valerie, "I'd have been at the airport to meet you."

"Is it too early in the day for a drink?" she asked. "I make a very good martini."

At that moment I came rather solidly down to earth. "You haven't listened to the radio or TV or seen a late afternoon newspaper?" I asked her.

"No," she said. "Should I?"

"Then you don't know that J. W. Sassoon is dead," I said.

She stood very still, very straight. I thought a dark shadow crossed over her eyes.

"The press and TV people have it that he died of a heart attack," I said. "The truth is he had a heart attack, but it was brought on while he was struggling for his life with a killer."

She gave me a cool, level stare, as if she was trying to read something more. "I think I'll have a Scotch on the rocks," she said. "It seems a little less frivolous than a martini. Will you join me, Mark?"

I said I would. She went over to the sideboard in the living room of her suite and made two drinks. I joined her there.

"You didn't come here to say welcome to New York," she said, handing me my glass.

"No. The police officer in charge of the case is a man named Hardy."

"Lieutenant Hardy!"

"He remembers you, of course."

The shadow darkened her eyes. "He's a good man who tried his best," she said.

"At a time that must have been very tough for you you made some hysterical threats against Sassoon," I said. "Something to the effect that you would get him if it took the rest of your life. Hardy remembers that, and now someone has polished off the old man. So it's just a coincidence that you are here in the hotel. Puzzling is the fact that J. W. Sassoon made your reservation at the Beaumont for you."

She sipped her Scotch—just sipped. "You came here to tell me that I'm a suspect?"

"To tell you that Hardy and Pierre Chambrun, my boss, would like to talk to you," I said. "Neither one of them is a conclusion-jumper."

"Would you believe me if I told you I didn't kill him?" she asked.

"Of course."

"Oh, I meant to 'get him,'" she said. She took another sip of her drink. "Not personally, Mark. Not with my own hands, or my own gun, or knife, or bottle of poison. I meant to find proof that he had Michael killed and turn that proof over to the police. Michael was my husband."

"I know."

"And so you're wondering how it happens that Sassoon made my hotel reservation for me?"

"I'm not wondering. I don't care why," I said. "But Chambrun and Hardy—" I was totally prepared to be her knight, ready to fight all the dragons in the world for her.

"You're very sweet," she said. She must have read my mind. "I suppose we'd better face the inquisition."

She took a look at herself in the glass over the sideboard, touched her rich red hair with the tips of her fingers, and then we went downstairs together to the second floor.

Miss Ruysdale gave Valerie that special look of appraisal that women reserve for each other. They had something in common, those two: a kind of pride, a kind of openness, a kind of courage.

"Mr. Clarke is with Mr. Chambrun and the Lieutenant," Ruysdale said.

Valerie's eyes widened. "Emory Clarke?"

"Yes."

Valerie looked toward the closed door of Chambrun's office. "This is turning out to be a very strange day," she said.

"Enemy?" I asked her.

She actually laughed. "Perhaps the only certain friend I have in the world," she said.

EMORY CLARKE WAS, as I have said, almost a ringer for the late Charles Laughton. He was a big man with thick iron-gray hair, carelessly brushed, heavy black eyebrows that curled and twisted and moved expressively when he spoke. His eyes were a pale blue, twinkling with humor and yet almost painfully penetrating when he looked at you. He made you feel revealed. His rather thick lips trembled with an anticipated grin which never quite developed. He was evidently a chain cigarette smoker, and ashes dribbled down the front of the three-hundred-dollar tropical worsted gray suit that looked as if he'd slept in it. This was a man who, in his political career, must have made many speeches and he used his voice like an actor. He made you listen.

He turned away from Chambrun as Valerie and I came into the office, and his tanned face—sunlamp-induced, I thought—lit up with genuine pleasure.

"My dear child! My dear Valerie!" he said.

She went quickly to him and he put his arm around her in a sort of paternal bear hug.

"Emory!" she said, and for a moment her red head rested against his shoulder.

They evidently had things to say to each other and I went into a brief huddle with Chambrun and Hardy. The Lieutenant looked worn.

"I've put out an APB on Johnny Sassoon," he told me. "Half the world seems to be looking for him. Heir to a huge fortune, controls of a complex business in his hands. Where do you think the sonofabitch can have got to?"

"No idea."

"Mrs. Brent knows what's up?" Chambrun asked.

"She didn't till I told her," I said. "Clarke is a good friend, she says."

She had turned away from Clarke and she was looking straight at Hardy. "Good afternoon, Lieutenant," she said.

"It would be nice to see you under pleasanter circumstances," Hardy said.

She turned away from him. "We met several years ago, Mr. Chambrun, when my husband and I stayed here," she said.

"One doesn't forget meeting you, Mrs. Brent."

"Let's not dwell on politeness," Valerie said. "I take it I'm a suspect."

"What nonsense!" Emory Clarke said.

"You're not suspected of physically smothering Sassoon," Hardy said.

"But?" Her eyes were fixed steadily on the detective.

"Just now I'm playing with any kind of loose ends I can find," Hardy said. "I know your history with Sassoon, Mrs. Brent. I know how certainly you believed he was responsible for your husband's death. I heard you threaten to keep after him if it took a lifetime. So you are here in this hotel he owns, your reservation made by him. It doesn't quite add up, Mrs. Brent."

Clarke's eyebrows arched. "I don't think you're required to answer questions, Val, without your lawyer present."

She stood so straight, her head held so high, like a heroine in a romantic novel. "I think perhaps I should explain now instead of later," she said. "I'd like to tell it when you're here, Emory, so that you'll understand."

"Let me guess," Clarke said, with that never-materializing smile twitching at the corner of his mouth. "'If you can't lick 'em, join 'em.' It just happens that I spent a couple of hours with J.W. only yesterday. We have—had—a mutual interest in certain matters connected with the so-called energy crisis. Oil. I am supposed to be a political expert in such matters. J.W. was somewhere near the top of the power structure. It so happened that when we came to the end of our business talk, he mentioned you, Val."

"Oh?"

"With pleasure." The smile almost arrived. "I suspect all men think of you with pleasure, my dear."

Old-world courtier, I thought.

"I doubt that I would think of Mrs. Brent with pleasure if she were out to get me," Chambrun said, his voice flat and cold.

"Ah, but that's just the point," Clarke said. "J.W. was pleased because Val had stopped being 'out to get him.'"

"Had she, now!" Chambrun said.

"He believed she had," Clarke said. "J.W. told me how fond he had been of both Val and Michael; how shocked and angered he had been by Michael's murder. He had put his own police force to work on the case."

"His own police force?" Hardy asked.

"He has a small squad of men who make the CIA and the FBI look like amateurs," Clarke said. "Not hampered by the law of the land or international treaties. Their techniques might make your blood run cold, Lieutenant. They did not, however, come up with Michael Brent's killer, J.W. told me. His other unhappiness was Val's conviction that he, J. W. Sassoon, was the villain of the piece. Imagine his delight, he told me, when he ran into Val at some sort of charity affair in London and he found that she had become convinced that she'd been wrong. The hatchet was buried. He'd always felt that he owed Michael money for the work he'd done on the book, and that now it was due Val. She'd refused from the beginning and still refused. But she had graciously allowed him to make her travel plans for her, her booking here at the Beaumont. He was like a kid with a new toy. Most charming woman, he called you, Val. A great pleasure not to have you on his enemies list.''

"He had an 'enemies list'?'' Hardy asked.

"I'm afraid I borrowed the phrase from our recent political scandals,'' Clarke said. He looked at Valerie, his eyes dancing. "But you were playing him for the big fall, weren't you, my dear?''

Valerie was looking straight at Clarke. "Yes,'' she said.

"A dangerous game,'' Clarke said, his eyebrows drawing together in a frown. "J.W. was a very tough cookie. You may have dazzled him for a bit with your charm, but very soon I think he'd have seen through you. Right about then I think you'd have wished you'd never been born. He'd have turned you over to the Wolves—my name for his army. He wasn't a forgiving man.''

"He chose violent punishment?'' Chambrun asked.

"I could give you a list of people I suspect displeased him,'' Clarke said. "They died in very unpleasant ways. A car accident, a hanging, a fire, shootings; all with an additional trademark—mutilation after death, or perhaps before death.''

"Like Michael," Valerie said. It was almost a whisper.

"I always suspected," Clarke said.

"You knew these things and you didn't go to the police?" Hardy asked.

"I didn't know anything, Lieutenant. I suspected. And I very much enjoy living, my friend. I respect you and your brothers in the law, but I may have even a deeper respect for the Wolves. The police of ten countries have never been able to lay a finger on them."

"Having told us this much, can you give us names?" Chambrun asked.

Clarke shrugged his broad shoulders. "I don't know any names, but I promise you, Mr. Chambrun, if I did I wouldn't tell you. A Turkish diplomat who considered talking, one guesses, wound up without his tongue."

"Does the name Mark Zorich mean anything to you?"

"A name only," Clarke said. "He sometimes conveyed messages for J.W. by phone. If he is one of the Wolves, Zorich is not really his name."

"You don't know him by sight?"

"No."

Chambrun shifted in his chair. "Who else has a private army, Mr. Clarke? It seems unlikely that Sassoon was murdered by his own troops."

Clarke took a crumpled package of cigarettes out of his pocket and lit one. "We live in a violent world, Mr. Chambrun," he said. He took a deep drag on his cigarette and let the smoke out in a curling spiral. "I'm not talking about burglaries, and rapes, and muggings, or even terrorist activities. There are power structures around the world bigger than governments. They take what they want by force. There is no such thing as privacy any longer. Phones are bugged, electronic listening devices are everywhere. People are spied on—their sex lives, their drinking habits, their tax returns, their medical histories. They are spied on by governments, by the military, by industrial espionage agents. Somewhere, in some complex computer, everything there is to know about you, Mr. Chambrun, is available, simply by pressing a series of buttons. We live in a society of bribery and blackmail.'' Clarke took another drag on his cigarette. ''When bribery or blackmail doesn't work, then the secret agents of the power structures turn to physical violence. Who else has a private army like the Wolves? There are dozens of them around the globe, Mr. Chambrun. J. W. Sassoon was on a collision course with most of them. Dog eat dog, man eat man. J.W. must have been living in a very rare moment for him, a moment—and I'm guessing it could only have been a matter of moments—when he was left unprotected.''

We were all silent for a moment, trying to take it in. Then Chambrun had another question.

''Do you know a man named Gamayel, Mr. Clarke?''

''Yes. He's an Iraqi diplomat. Staying here at the hotel.''

"He claims he was trying to negotiate a deal with Sassoon. That some top secret papers he left with Sassoon are missing."

Clarke pursed his thick lips. "He could be talking about the biggest oil deal of our time. It could shift the balances of power in a startling fashion."

The office door opened and Miss Ruysdale stepped in. "Sorry to interrupt, Mr. Chambrun," she said. "Mr. Carlson is here and he says it's urgent."

Carlson hadn't waited. He was right behind her in the doorway. He looked ghastly. He didn't wait for an invitation.

"I must talk to you and Lieutenant Hardy alone," he said to Chambrun. He turned. "I'm sorry, Emory—Val."

Clarke looked at Valerie. "I'll buy you a drink in the Trapeze Bar," he said.

"I'll still want to talk to you, Mrs. Brent," Hardy said.

"Of course."

I watched her go with Clarke. It was as if someone had turned off a light in the room.

Carlson's hands were shaking as he tried to light a cigarette. "I had a phone call at the office," he said. "Johnny Sassoon has been kidnapped. They're asking for a half million in cash. Instructions will come on how to deliver it. Police not to be involved."

"I am the police," Hardy said.

"You were excepted, Lieutenant. You are instructed to call off your search for Johnny if we expect to see him alive."

"You can raise the money?" Hardy asked.

"No problem. You will back off, Lieutenant?"

Hardy brought his fist down on the arm of his chair. "Listening to you and Clarke, Mr. Carlson, I get the feeling you think a police officer is some kind of a midget!"

"What can we do except follow instructions?" Carlson asked. "I don't mind telling you that if anything happens to Johnny before he gets straightened away in his new responsibilities, you may see the biggest financial disaster of this or any other time."

"The boy himself doesn't matter?" Chambrun asked, his tone cold.

"Of course he matters," Carlson said.

"Where and when are you to receive your instructions?" Chambrun asked.

"Here at the hotel—in Johnny's room. I'm to be there at seven o'clock with the money and wait."

Chambrun reached out for the house phone on his desk and told the switchboard to locate Jerry Dodd and get him up here on the double. "Doesn't it strike you as odd that the contact should be made here?" he asked Carlson after he'd put down the phone.

"I hadn't thought," Carlson said. "I suppose—"

"I suppose Jerry Dodd, our security man, is going to find another bug in that room," Chambrun interrupted. I'd seldom seen him angry. "They've turned this hotel into a crime center! You're to use that room so that they can overhear what you may say to me, or the police, or anyone else who might be with you while you wait for their call." He glanced at his watch. "It's five o'clock. Do you have to go back downtown for the money?"

"Don Webster, with a couple of our men to guard him, is supposed to bring it to me here, in your office. They should be arriving soon." Carlson pressed the tips of his fingers against his eyes for a moment. "How much chance do you think there is of getting Johnny back, Mr. Chambrun?"

"I couldn't begin to guess," Chambrun said. "Why was he snatched in the first place? The people who are bugging my hotel, the big-time enemies of J. W. Sassoon, don't need money."

"Who doesn't need a half million dollars?" Hardy muttered.

"It's a respectable-sounding figure to make it seem real," Chambrun said. "My guess is they've threatened Johnny, told him what it is he must do for them. Are there decisions he can make, Carlson, in spite of advice from you, or from trustees or boards of directors?"

"J.W. had absolute control of all that matters," Carlson said. "He could overrule anyone in his enormous complex of businesses. He was the final word. Quite simply, Johnny has inherited that control."

"Strange that J.W. would leave that power in the hands of someone he knew was totally incompetent," Chambrun said.

"I pleaded with him for the last year or more to set up some kind of a control board to handle things till Johnny was equipped," Carlson said.

"He refused?"

"He laughed at me," Carlson said. "He told me the only thing he regretted was that he wasn't going to be around to enjoy the kind of madhouse Johnny was certain to put in motion. He thought of it as a big joke."

Chambrun took a cigarette from his silver case. He turned it round and round in his stubby fingers, making no move to light it.

"What happens to the business structure if Johnny should turn up dead—say tonight or tomorrow?" he asked.

Carlson moistened his lips. "Then there is a control board that would take over—consisting of the heads of the ten biggest companies under the conglomerate umbrella. I am the legal counsel to that board as I was to J.W."

"The chairman of that board?" Chambrun asked.

"He will be elected at their first meeting—if they meet," Carlson said.

"It's an interesting situation," Chambrun said. He paused to light his cigarette. "J. W. Sassoon is murdered. Johnny Sassoon is, perhaps kidnapped, perhaps also murdered. Vast power passes into other hands. How hungry have the members of this control board been to take over from J. W. Sassoon?"

Carlson reached out to the back of a chair to steady himself. "He was King. He was a despot," Carlson said. "These other men are big fish in their fields, Mr. Chambrun. There has been jealousy. There has been outright conflict. But the simple truth is that J. W. Sassoon never made a mistake that I know of, never made a wrong judgment. Under his control they all grew richer and more powerful, year after year. They may have hated his guts personally, but they had to recognize his genius."

"But one or all of them could have decided that the time had come for power to change hands. What I'm saying is that Sassoon could have been killed by his own associates." Chambrun watched the pale blue smoke curl up from the end of his cigarette. "What role does Emory Clarke play in this power structure, Mr. Carlson?"

Carlson's knuckles showed white as he gripped the back of the chair. "He knows more about the political setups in the oil countries around the world than any other man alive. He is the adviser on such matters to the conglomerate, paid a very high retainer. A brilliant man."

"With Sassoon dead he might become even more valuable, might he not? Command an even higher retainer?"

"I suppose that could be," Carlson said. "He advised J.W., but J.W. didn't always follow his advice. J.W. was smarter than anyone else, including Emory. Johnny would certainly have to lean heavily on Emory."

"And so would the control board—if Johnny doesn't get back into the picture." Chambrun put down his cigarette in the silver ash tray beside him. "You asked me a question a while back, Mr. Carlson; how much chance do I think there is of getting Johnny back alive? I would say a very small chance."

Jerry Dodd turned up then, before the full implication of what Chambrun had been saying had really begun to percolate. Chambrun brought Jerry up to date.

"My feeling is that the reason they've chosen Johnny's room as the place for the contact to be made is that it's bugged," Chambrun said.

"Sonofabitch!" Jerry said. He started for the door.

"Hold it, Jerry. If it's the same little transistor gimmick, located in the phone, if you monkey around with it, won't they be aware of it if they're listening?"

"Yes, they would."

"Isn't there another way to check?" Chambrun asked. "Didn't the switchboard hear something odd on Sassoon's line?"

"True."

"Then let's alert Mrs. Veach, and then call Johnny's room. The Woodson girl is waiting for him there. When she talks into the phone, Mrs. Veach will pick up the sound, if there is a sound."

Jerry called the switchboard and laid it out for Mrs. Veach. While he was waiting for her to set up, Jerry turned to Chambrun. "What do I say to the Woodson girl, in case they're listening?"

"Play it straight," Chambrun said. "Tell her Johnny's been kidnapped and that Mr. Carlson is coming to the room to wait for a call with instructions on how to deliver the ransom. If she mentions police, say they've been called off."

It was all clear enough, except that when Mrs. Veach rang Johnny's room, Trudy Woodson didn't answer.

"She doesn't stay put anywhere very long," Jerry said.

I reminded him that she hadn't answered the phone the last time we'd called, but we'd found her hiding under a sheet on Johnny's bed when we went down there. "She doesn't answer the phone unless she feels like it."

"Go up and let yourself in the room, Jerry," Chambrun said. "If she's there, give it to her straight—remembering that you're probably being heard. Then call me from the room and Mrs. Veach can check out the line."

Jerry had only just left when Webster, the Ivy League character from Carlson's office, turned up with a large black suitcase and two men who were bodyguards from a special security service. Being in the same room with half a million dollars in cash gave me an odd feeling. Webster and the guards left, and Chambrun began discussing a game plan with Carlson and Hardy.

"We still have no idea how things are set up here in the hotel," Chambrun said. "These bugging devices indicate they've had a pretty free hand for some time. God knows how many people are hanging around the hallways, watching. I think you ought to appear to pull out of this, Hardy. You've got to call off your APB on Johnny. I don't think you should be seen going to Johnny's room with Carlson and me."

Hardy nodded slowly. He had that kind of stupid look on his broad face that I knew was a mask. "If they've done in that boy, so help me God—"

"Let's face the facts of life," Chambrun said. "You take one step inside the circle they've drawn around themselves—Sassoon's people or some other group— you're facing power that can send you to pounding a beat on Staten Island! I think there are just two possibilities. Sassoon's own people are grabbing for control, or another adversary group sees a chance to deal if Sassoon and his son are out of the way. Either way there are two ways of handling Johnny. Dead, there are new leaders to deal with, a new set of values. Alive, if he has been sufficiently terrorized, he will do what they tell him—an extra advantage, since he has the power of absolute decisions. Right, Carlson?''

Carlson nodded.

''So if Johnny has been properly scared, we'll see him alive, but under someone's thumb. If he's tried to play the hero, we're not likely to be able to do much more than go to his funeral.'' Chambrun's bright eyes fixed on Carlson. ''You know Johnny. Can you make a guess about him?''

Carlson shook his head. ''The silly young bastard is a born hero without the equipment to make it stick,'' he said.

The phone rang. It was Jerry Dodd calling from Johnny-baby's room. Trudy Woodson had not waited for her boy friend. I imagined she'd found someone else to take care of her late afternoon sex needs. As soon as Jerry cut off, Chambrun checked with Mrs. Veach. The phone in Johnny's room was probably bugged. There were the strange noises on the line she'd heard from J. W. Sassoon's room.

Chambrun glanced at his watch. ''We might as well go up there and wait,'' he said.

It was six-thirty.

Hardy pulled himself wearily up out of his chair. "Don't keep it a secret when it happens," he said. "I'll be around. There are a few things I can check."

Chambrun, Carlson and I went up to the twelfth floor, Carlson carrying the bag with the money.

"Once in the room, we don't speculate," Chambrun said. "We're waiting for the call, we're anxious for Johnny. Period. Just bear in mind someone is hearing every damn thing we say."

It was spooky waiting in Johnny's room, knowing that someone could hear you if you hiccoughed. Chambrun talked a little—about how we could count on Hardy pulling out, and how we must follow instructions to the letter if we hoped to get Johnny back.

At precisely seven o'clock the phone rang. That was it. Carlson answered.

I could only hear his end of the conversation, but we got it from him afterwards. Did he have the money? He did. Was Trudy Woodson with us? She was not. She, Carlson was told, would be the messenger. She was to take the money and go to a public phone booth at the corner of Fifth Avenue and 59th Street. She would answer the phone when it rang—which would be at exactly eight o'clock. Carlson said if we couldn't find Trudy, he would bring the money himself. That wouldn't do, he was told. Trudy must bring it. Trudy was Johnny's girl. She would follow instructions without hesitation because Johnny mattered to her. But if she couldn't be found? Tough luck. Would they call back if she couldn't be found to go to the phone booth? They would have to regroup, reconsider. Carlson had better damn well find her.

When Carlson put down the phone, he looked sick. He told us the orders, gasping for breath like a fish out of water.

"How do we find her?" he asked.

"She's in and out of your office, according to you," Chambrun said. "Where does she live?"

"No idea," Carlson said.

"Phone book," Chambrun said. And while I looked in the directory, he was on the phone, giving orders to have the hotel searched for Trudy. She could be in one of the bars, one of the restaurants.

She wasn't listed in the Manhattan telephone book. Carlson said he thought she'd once dated the Ivy League character, Don Webster, but Webster didn't answer his home phone and he hadn't gone back to the office after delivering the money.

There was a bottle of bourbon, half full, on Johnny-baby's bureau. Carlson went over and poured some in a water tumbler. He looked as if he needed it. He tasted it, made a face, and crossed the room to the bathroom door, obviously to dilute it. He opened the door and went in.

If you have ever heard a grown man scream, you know what a shattering sound it is. Carlson screamed—and screamed again. Chambrun beat me to the bathroom door, but I was directly behind him and I could see over his shoulder.

I remember I staggered away, not wanting to look a second longer than I had to. Trudy Woodson was lying, naked, in the bathtub. There was a round, black hole between her eyes, obviously a gunshot wound. And her naked body, her breasts and her stomach, had been slashed and gouged at by some kind of knife. The tub was red with her blood.

Carlson was on his hands and knees in front of the toilet bowl, throwing up his guts.

PART TWO

ONE

TRUDY WOODSON HAD, according to the Medical Examiner, been dead for several hours. The last time we had seen her alive was when she'd barged into Chambrun's office a little after three that afternoon, approximately four hours before we found her in that bloody bathtub. Just when she had gone to Johnny-baby's room after she'd left Chambrun's office we were trying to check out. There had been no signs of any struggle in the room. An educated guess was that someone had been waiting for her and shot her between the eyes when she let herself into the room. She had then been carried into the bathroom, her dress removed, and her naked body lowered into the tub. Trudy hadn't worn anything under her dress. The poor little idiot had been always ready for action. The dress, her sandals, and her handbag had been found under the washbasin. Once she had been lowered into the tub, she had been methodically butchered.

But I'm getting ahead of myself.

As I've said, I got away from the sight of it as quickly as I could, leaving Chambrun and the retching Carlson in the bathroom. My first impulse was to call Jerry Dodd, try to locate Lieutenant Hardy. I reached for the phone beside the bed, and then drew back my hand. The tiny transistor we thought was there must have conveyed plenty to listening ears.

Carlson's screaming could have shattered eardrums. I realized I was in shock. I couldn't make myself think clearly how to handle things.

Chambrun came out of the bathroom, the awful sound of Carlson's vomiting behind him. Chambrun's face looked gray, set in hard, angular lines like a marble mask. His eyes glittered with a kind of fury I don't think I'd ever seen before. He walked stiffly toward the phone as if his knee joints were half locked. I don't think he knew I was there.

He picked up the phone and, in a strange voice I'd never heard before, he asked Mrs. Veach to find Jerry Dodd and Hardy. Then he spoke as if someone else had come on the phone. I realized he was talking to whoever was tuned in on the transistor.

"The Woodson girl can't deliver the money," he said. "She's been murdered. You sonofabitches will have to come up with another plan." He jammed down the receiver on its cradle. He turned to me. He was breathing hard, as if he couldn't get air into his lungs. "I think you'd better go down to that phone booth on Fifty-ninth Street, Mark. When it rings, you answer it and tell them what's happened. You've got about thirty-five minutes."

"What's the point? You just told them," I said.

"We can't be certain that the kidnappers are on the other end of that transistor," he said. "If they are, they'll know you're heading for the booth. If they aren't and there's nobody to answer when they call, we may be placing Johnny in danger. We can't risk that. Give them my private unlisted number. This room is going to be no place to talk to them from."

"And if they're listening right now?" I asked.

Chambrun looked at the phone. "My private number is 232-6668," he said, loud and clear. Then: "Get going, Mark."

I was glad to go. It may have been imagination, but I thought I was aware of the sick, sweet smell of blood. I took an elevator down to the lobby. I had the cockeyed notion that anyone who looked at me could see what I knew reflected in my face.

I was almost at the Fifth Avenue entrance when I saw Hardy come through the revolving door. There was a smart-looking woman with him. He stopped, but he didn't introduce me.

"You make contact?" he asked.

I nodded.

"What the hell's the matter with you?" he asked.

"Trudy Woodson was supposed to deliver the money," I said. "She can't. Somebody shot her between the eyes, dumped her in the bathtub in Johnny's room, and cut her to pieces. I'm going to an outside phone where they said they'd call."

Hardy's pale blue eyes were cold as two newly minted dimes. "Michael Brent!" he said, almost inaudible.

For the first time it penetrated. Trudy had been killed in much the same way I'd heard Michael Brent's murder described.

"Chambrun's up there," I said. "He's sent out a call for you. I've got to hurry."

I don't think the woman with Hardy had heard much of what we'd said. She'd moved away when she saw Hardy wasn't going to introduce us. Hardy just nodded. He headed quickly toward the elevators. He seemed to have forgotten the woman. She watched him go, looking puzzled.

I went out onto the street. It was just five blocks to the phone booth the kidnappers had mentioned. It was easier to walk it, or jog it, than to try to get a cab in the early evening traffic.

People on the street looked so normal! Couples walked together in the twilight along the edge of the park across the way. I wondered how they'd have looked if they'd been aware of that bloody tragedy in a hotel room just a few yards away. I wondered how I looked. Like something out of a horror novel?

I saw the glass booth long before I reached it. I began to run toward it. I didn't want someone else to take it over. I saw a man pause outside it and I almost shouted at him not to use it. He evidently changed his mind and strolled away.

I got to it and went in, closing the door. It was six minutes to eight. I lifted the receiver but kept my finger on the hook, holding it down. I meant it to look as though I was talking in case someone wanted to use it.

Sweat was running down inside my clothes. I couldn't shake the picture of Trudy, so full of life and energy only a few hours ago. I found it difficult to concentrate on Johnny Sassoon and his problem. "Poison," Chambrun had called Trudy. Whatever she was, no one rated that kind of violence. As I watched the minute hand on my watch creep toward the hour, I could feel the sensations of shock and daze slowly fading, and in their place there was anger. I wanted to help square Trudy's account, but how could you square it without becoming the same kind of uncivilized bastard yourself? Going to prison for Murder-one was too good for the monster who'd carved up Trudy's lovely young body. There must be some kind of exquisite torture you could inflict on that kind of creep.

The phone rang.

I took my finger off the hook and spoke quickly. "I'm here in place of Trudy Woodson," I said.

There was a kind of mumbling sound on the other end.

"Listen to me while I explain why—in case you don't already know. Trudy Woodson is dead. Somebody knocked her off. I'm Mark Haskell, one of Pierre Chambrun's people. Do you hear me? Do you understand?"

No one spoke, but I could hear a kind of heavy, labored breathing on the other end.

"Trudy is dead," I repeated. "I came for new instructions."

Only the breathing, sounding like an old, old man fighting for survival.

"I have a telephone number for you," I said. "It's Chambrun's private, unlisted number. Someone will be waiting for you to call if you can't give me instructions now. It's a clear line, not bugged. Are you listening?"

There was a kind of strangling cough at the other end, no more.

"The number is 232-6668." I said it slowly and then repeated it.

The breathing stopped. The dial tone buzzed in my ear. That was all. The man on the other end hadn't uttered a single word. I stepped out of the phone booth which had become an oven while I waited in it. My shirt and undershirt were wringing wet.

It occurred to me that I might not have been talking to the kidnapper at all. Someone unconnected might have called that number expecting to reach someone else, and listened, without comment, to my story. The kidnapper could have called and gotten a busy signal. I waited a good five minutes for the phone to ring again, but it didn't.

I headed back for the Beaumont.

THE MOMENT I STEPPED INTO the hotel's air-conditioned lobby, I sensed something abnormal. Have you ever walked into your home and been instantly aware that something was wrong, a piece of furniture out of place, even a stranger in your kitchen—who turns out to be a repair man let in by your landlord? There was something wrong with the Beaumont, which was my home. It took me a moment to realize what it was.

There were people in the lobby who didn't belong there. What made them look out of place? It was a kind of instinct, I guess. Something I did almost every night of my life was to cruise around the hotel, into the bars and restaurants and the Blue Lagoon nightclub. I was looking for people who might have some publicity value for us or who might need special attention from the management. Shelda, my sometime girl, used to say I was like Marshal Dillon putting Dodge City to bed every night. I guess the marshal would have had an eye for strangers in town. I had the same instinct for out-of-place people in the Beaumont. We had over fifteen hundred guests in residence most of the time and I didn't know them all by sight; couldn't possibly. But they are all rich, they all have a certain style. Some of them are for real and some of them fake it, but none of them wear fifty-dollar suits out of a factory warehouse. Tonight there were eight or ten out-of-place guys in the lobby. They had cop written all over them.

I spotted Mike Maggio, the night bell captain, and flagged him.

"Any luck?" he asked. Mike is a dark, curly-haired Italian with mischief written all over him under normal circumstances. Tonight he was almost comically serious.

"Maybe," I said. "I'm not dead sure."

"The boss cut me in on what's happening, or I'd have been trying to give all these cops the bum's rush." His normally smiling mouth tightened. "I guess she was a little bit of a tramp," he said. "She was Johnny-baby's girl, but she had an eye for anyone else who might be available. Me, for instance. Not screwing the hotel guests is a rule I don't break. I wish I had. And I hope I get my hands on the sonofabitch who did it to her. We Sicilians know how to handle a knife, too." He drew a deep breath. "The boss is still up on the twelfth floor. You're to report to him there."

I started for the elevators and found myself confronted by the woman who'd come into the hotel earlier with Hardy.

"Forgive me for stopping you," she said. "Do you remember? I came into the hotel a little while ago with Lieutenant Hardy."

"I remember," I said.

"Do you expect to see him? I think he may have forgotten about me."

"I may see him."

"He wanted me to identify someone for him," the woman said. I spotted her for a genuine lady who'd come on hard times. "I work in Charlene's Boutique on Park Avenue. My name is Emily Wilson. I was to look at a woman who may have bought some things there yesterday."

"I'll tell him you're still here," I said.

"I saw the woman," she said. "She just went into the main dining room with an elderly gentleman."

The sweat on my body felt suddenly clammy. A boutique, the black underthings in J. W. Sassoon's room, a woman in the company of an elderly gentleman. "I have to get back to my family," the woman said. "My children will be wondering what on earth's happened to me."

"The things the woman bought—black lace negligee, bra, panties, slippers?" I asked. My mouth felt dry.

"You know about it?"

"Will you point your customer out to me?" I asked. "I may know her and it will save your having to wait for Hardy."

We went across the lobby to the main dining room. I told the headwaiter I was just looking for someone, didn't want a table. The room was pretty well thinned

out; theater-goers were long gone, the people who
wanted entertainment would have chosen the Blue
Lagoon.

I saw them at once—Valerie Brent and Emory
Clarke. Clarke was studying the menu. Valerie, smiling, was illustrating some anecdote with eloquent
hands. I let the lady from the boutique do her own
looking, but I knew it was as inevitable as a Greek
tragedy.

"The one with the dark red hair; the older man
giving his order to the waiter," the boutique lady said.

"I know her," I said. "I'll tell Lieutenant Hardy.
He'll let you know in case he needs you for an official
identification."

The lady thanked me and left. I stood there looking across the room at Valerie, still involved with her
animated story. She would never have considered a
sexual romp with a gross old bastard like J. W. Sassoon. Or would she? Would she have gone that far as
part of a plan to "get" him?

JOHNNY-BABY'S ROOM on the twelfth floor was
crowded with people, all official except Chambrun
and an ashen-faced Raymond Carlson. There were
fingerprint men and photographers and people from
the Medical Examiner's office. There was Hardy and
his man Kramer. There were two white-coated young
men with a stretcher. They hadn't taken Trudy away
yet.

Carlson was sitting on the edge of the bed, bent
forward as if he had a stomach ache. I reported to

Chambrun what had happened at the phone booth on Fifty-ninth Street.

"Anything else?" he asked me.

For the first time in all the years I'd worked for him, I lied to him. Without thinking about it, I had decided to obstruct justice for a little while, at least. I told Chambrun there was nothing. The black lace things could have nothing to do with Trudy's death, I told myself. Trudy had, for the moment, taken priority over J. W. Sassoon, I told myself.

Chambrun put his hand on Carlson's shoulder. "You'd better go down to my office and wait for a phone call," he said. "You're not any more use here."

"Thank God!" Carlson said, and got unsteadily to his feet.

"Go down with him, Mark. Have Ruysdale set him up in my office," Chambrun said. "Then make the rounds downstairs. Everyone's been alerted. We're still looking for Mark Zorich and James Olin—if they are two people. The maid who knows Olin by sight is stationed in the lobby."

"Anything new here?" I asked him.

Chambrun was still wearing that angry, stone face. "A coincidence that may become more than a coincidence when it's tested out," he said. "The girl was shot with the same caliber bullet that killed Michael Brent two years ago. Ballistics may show it's from the same gun. Since Hardy couldn't identify the owner of the gun then, it's not much more than a curiosity now. Get moving, you two. That phone call may come any minute."

Carlson and I started for the door.

"The money, you idiots!" Chambrun shouted at us.

We'd been prepared to leave half a million dollars lying around like old laundry. I picked up the bag, surprised that it didn't seem heavier. I thought of half a million dollars being a mountain of gold.

Carlson had nothing to say on the way down to the office. He still seemed to be in shock, reaching out ahead of him as he walked, like a blind man.

Miss Ruysdale was on the job when we got there—long after her regular hours. She was always on the job when she was needed. We took Carlson into Chambrun's office and pointed out to him which of the four phones on Chambrun's desk was 232-6668.

"There's no ring, Mr. Carlson," Ruysdale explained. "Just a little red light on the base of the instrument shows. None of the other phones will light up. They're routed through me."

I couldn't be sure Carlson heard her, took it in. He sat down in Chambrun's chair, staring straight ahead at the wall.

"The minute you get a call with instructions," I said, "have Miss Ruysdale connect you with the boss."

He didn't answer.

"Carlson! Are you listening?"

He lifted his bloodshot eyes to me, and two tears ran down his pale cheeks. "You saw her!" he said. "Oh, my God!" He looked at Ruysdale. "Thank God you didn't, Miss Ruysdale. No one should have had to see her. It will stay with me until I die."

Ruysdale's answer was to go over to the sideboard and pour him a stiff slug of Jack Daniels on the rocks.

She brought it back to him. "You've understood the instructions about the phone and what to do after you get the call, Mr. Carlson?" she asked in a matter-of-fact voice. There was no vestige of pity or sympathy. She was right, of course. All that was needed to drop him off the deep end was sympathy.

"Johnny's life may depend on your making sense," I said.

"I know," he said dully, staring at the wall once more.

Ruysdale and I went out to her office.

"You better keep an eye on him," I said. "He may not even answer the god-damned thing if the light blinks."

She nodded and pointed to the phones on her desk. "It shows out here," she said. "I'll know if he doesn't pick up."

Somehow I wanted to share what was on my mind with her. She was so much wiser than most of us. But I couldn't risk the contempt I was sure she'd feel for me for ever thinking of protecting Valerie Brent ahead of Chambrun. I didn't tell her, and I started downstairs feeling like a noble heel.

Valerie and Clarke were still at their table in the main dining room. I set sail across the room and they saw me coming.

"You're just in time to join us in a brandy," Clarke said.

I decided I could use one, and I sat down with them.

"Chambrun's chef is, as usual, super-excellent," Clarke said.

I looked at them, cheerful and relaxed, and realized that unless they were the prize actors of all time, they didn't know about Johnny's kidnapping or about Trudy. They'd left Chambrun's office before Carlson told us about the kidnapping; they'd spent the last couple of hours having cocktails in the Trapeze and then having dinner here. If they'd known, they'd have been bombarding me with questions.

I took a sip of the brandy the waiter brought me before I let them have both barrels. Valerie seemed to freeze where she was sitting when I got to Trudy. She didn't need to be reminded of the similarity to Michael Brent's murder. I mentioned the thing about the similarity of the bullets.

Emory Clarke listened with a scowling intentness, his mobile eyebrows moving in shock and surprise as I made point after point.

"It's unbelievable," Valerie whispered when I'd finished.

Clarke cupped his hands around his brandy glass. "It's part of a pattern that most people believe is unbelievable," he said. "When you learn the reason for it, you'll find it fits a pattern. What does Trudy Woodson have to do with a big business power struggle? She knew something—perhaps something she had no idea was important. Perhaps she didn't even know she knew it!"

Valerie's voice was unsteady. "The thing I never understood about Michael," she said, "was the cutting up—afterwards."

Clarke shrugged. "Trademark," he suggested.

"Whose?" I asked.

Clarke reached out a big, freckled hand and put it down gently over one of Valerie's. "It wasn't meant to mean anything to you, Val," he said, "any more than the Woodson girl's mutilation is meant to mean anything to us, sitting here at this table. But it means something to someone."

"It just doesn't make sense!" Valerie said. "Senseless brutality! Some kind of maniac, I always have thought."

"A signature for someone who knows how to read it," Clarke said. He fished a cigarette out of his pocket and lit it, his eyes narrowed against the smoke.

I took another sip of my brandy. It burned going down. I had to get to my nobility.

"I've got to get back on the job," I said, "but I have something to tell you, Mrs. Brent."

"Val," she said.

"Val." I took another sip, put my glass down, and took the plunge. "There are some details about J. W. Sassoon's death that haven't been made public. Some things we found in his room—women's things. A negligee, underwear, slippers."

Clarke laughed. "J.W. had himself a girl? Now that's news!"

Valerie didn't laugh. Her hazel eyes were fixed on me, widened, I thought.

"The things that were found were brand new," I said. "They were bought just yesterday at a place called Charlene's Boutique on Park Avenue. Hardy has a witness who will testify that you bought them, Val. Hardy doesn't know it yet, but this witness pointed you out to me a few minutes ago. I am supposed to tell Hardy. I—I wanted to tell you first.''

She seemed to be about to say something, but it didn't happen at once. Clarke was staring at her, his bushy eyebrows raised. Cigarette ash dribbled down onto his necktie, unnoticed.

"There was a black negligee, black bra and panties, and a pair of black slippers," I said.

Val looked at me straight on, not faltering. "I bought exactly these things at Charlene's yesterday," she said.

I felt deflated. I'd wanted her to deny it. I'd wanted her to make a liar out of the saleswoman.

"But they were stolen from me," Valerie said.

"Stolen?" Clarke's voice was sharp.

"It was a beautiful day," she said. I had the uncomfortable feeling that those wide eyes were studying me, trying to guess whether I was buying. "I bought those things at Charlene's and walked over from Park to Fifth Avenue—just across the way from the Beaumont. The sunshine was warm and pleasant. The air seemed less polluted than usual. There were flowers in the park—and children playing. Two years ago Michael and I used to sit there in the park talking about his work, and about us, and about life in general. Somehow, yesterday, I wanted to relive one of those moments. I went into the park and sat down on a bench, the package from Charlene's beside me. I was watching some kids throwing a frisbee back and forth. I—I was thinking about Michael and the job I'd set myself to do. Then—then someone came up behind me, grabbed my package, and took off! I—I was startled. I turned round on the bench and saw a tall man racing off with my package. He was running away from me—back to me. I never saw his face— only a bright red and yellow sports shirt and white buckskin shoes."

She stopped, her eyes pleading with me to believe her.

"You reported it?" Clarke asked. He was a practical man.

"I looked around for a policeman," Val said, "but, as usual when you want one, there wasn't one."

"But you eventually found one and reported it?" Clarke persisted. He wanted her clean just as I wanted her clean.

"No," she said. It was almost a whisper. "I—I just didn't want to get involved in all the red tape, Emory. Filling out a complaint, perhaps having to appear in court. I was angry, but the loss wasn't that important."

"Did you tell anybody about it—yesterday?" Clarke asked.

"Who would I tell? Why would I tell? I mean, it was an irritating thing, but not life and death."

"Hardy will have to make something of it," Clarke said. More ashes fell down the front of his suit.

"I have to tell him," I said.

"I understand that, Mark," Val said. "What I don't understand is how those things wound up in J.W.'s room."

"Your man in the sports shirt wasn't a casual thief," Clarke said. "He knew who you were, what was in the package. He intended to frame you. Had you been aware that anyone was following you?"

"No!" Val looked at me. "You believe me, don't you, Mark?"

I must have been registering doubt and concern. Her story was too pat, too unprovable. "What matters is whether Hardy believes you," I said.

TWO

I FOUND HARDY AND CHAMBRUN still in Johnny-baby's room. Poor little Trudy was gone, along with the Medical Examiner's crew, who would probably cut her up some more performing an autopsy, digging for the bullet in her brain.

I told Hardy that his saleswoman had identified Val as the buyer of the things at Charlene's. I didn't tell him that I'd forewarned Val or what her story was. I was still not being quite honest. I made it sound as though I'd run into the woman after I'd taken Carlson down to Chambrun's office, not before. I didn't say that in so many words, but since I hadn't reported it before, they took it for granted—I thought!

Chambrun was looking at Hardy, a little smile moving the corners of his angry mouth. "You expected that, Hardy?" he asked.

The Lieutenant shrugged. "You play all the angles. Mrs. Brent is here in the hotel, out to 'get' Sassoon. She is the kind of woman who would shop at Charlene's. It's a high-class joint, expensive. It was worth checking out. Funny, but in a way I hoped it wouldn't."

"There may be an explanation," I said.

Hardy's tired eyes looked straight at me. "Is that what she told you?" he asked.

I think I stammered, "Told me?"

"You're the worst goddam liar in the whole United States," Hardy said, not angry.

I didn't dare look at Chambrun, but he was looking at me. I could feel his eyes burn. "You warned her, Mark?" he asked.

No answer was an answer.

"I'm not psychic," Hardy said, still quite amiable. "The lobby is crawling with my men. They saw you talk to Mrs. Wilson, the woman from the boutique, and they saw her point out Mrs. Brent to you. You came upstairs and didn't say anything to us. I figured you'd turned romantic and noble on us." He chuckled. "Then I just heard you'd been talking to her in the dining room. What's her story?"

"She admits she bought the things at Charlene's," I said, still not looking at Chambrun. "She was sitting in the park with the package beside her on the bench, watching some kids throwing a frisbee, when some guy snatched the package and ran. She didn't report it because she could afford the loss and didn't want to get involved in all the red tape of a complaint."

"Could be, I suppose," Hardy said.

"Did she try to stop the thief?" Chambrun asked.

I made myself took at him. "I'm sorry, boss," I said. "I'm afraid Mrs. Brent was a little heady for me. She's been through such a lot. I—I don't know if she tried to stop the thief. She says he was wearing a loud sports shirt and white bucks. She says she didn't see his face."

I think I expected Chambrun to point dramatically to the door, tell me to pack my things and leave the hotel forever. Instead there was the tiniest quirk of a smile at the corner of his mouth. "It's been a rather sexy day for you, friend," he said. "Perhaps when the children are playing with their friends again tomorrow, they might remember having seen something. It would help to confirm."

Hardy grinned at me. "Try to play on our team, will you, Mark?" The grin faded. "Evidently the kidnappers haven't called back. No word from Carlson or Miss Ruysdale." He looked at Chambrun, as if for help. "I keep trying to fit the two murders and the kidnapping into one frame. It won't work, somehow."

Chambrun had turned bleak again. "Michael Brent was shot and cut up two years ago," he said. "Tonight this girl, shot and cut up. Same method, same signposts. J. W. Sassoon wasn't shot or cut up—killed in an entirely different way. Johnny Sassoon may have been kidnapped, may have been killed. Different technique again. It looks to me as if the Beaumont has been turned into a battleground for two opposing forces. Well—" and he drew a deep breath "—I won't have it!"

"We should be getting fingerprint reports back from Washington soon—the ones we couldn't identify in Sassoon's room," Hardy said. "Meanwhile, there are still the two men, Zorich and Olin, to find. What do you make out of the kidnappers' silence?"

"Either the person Mark heard breathing into the telephone wasn't one of them, or Trudy Woodson's murder made some difference to them. After all, they had named her as the go-between to deliver the money.

Change of plans. Who knows?'' Chambrun took a cigarette from his case and lit it. "I'll cooperate in every way I can, Hardy, but by God, I'm going to set up my own defenses here in the hotel. I have fifteen hundred guests to protect—and a reputation I cherish. Any more of this and we'll have a mass panic on our hands."

THE KIND OF PANIC Chambrun was talking about was likely to hit the fan the next morning when the news of Trudy Woodson's murder leaked to the media. J. W. Sassoon's death had been reported as a heart attack, nothing to distress any of the hotel guests. But the gory details of Trudy's murder would have the place in an uproar.

It was a little after nine o'clock when Chambrun and I got back to his office. Miss Ruysdale reported no in-calls on the private line. Carlson, she reported, seemed to be in a kind of trance. She had looked in on him from time to time and he just sat at Chambrun's desk staring at the wall. Mr. Gamayel, the Iraqi, had called half a dozen times to find out if there was any news of his precious documents.

We went into Chambrun's office and found Carlson just as Ruysdale had described him. He didn't seem to hear us come in. He sat staring at the wall like a man in a dream. He didn't move until Chambrun touched him on the shoulder.

"Oh, it's you," he said. He waved vaguely at the desk. "Nothing."

"What you need is some rest—some sleep," Chambrun said.

"I couldn't sleep," Carlson said. "I'd see her the minute I closed my eyes. I may see her for the rest of my life. God help me, Mr. Chambrun, I've got to tell someone. I—I may be responsible for what happened to that child. I keep trying to tell myself I'm not. And yet—" His voice trailed off.

"How could you possibly be responsible?" Chambrun asked very quietly. Carlson was so close to smashing into a thousand pieces he had to be handled gently.

"It's all so complex," Carlson said. "I've spent my entire adult life working for J. W. Sassoon. It's like operating in a maze. You walk into it, a reasonably innocent young man, and you find yourself in the center of undreamed-of complications, maneuverings, bottom dealings, power plays. It's like a giant war game with big battles around every corner."

"About Trudy Woodson and why you think you may be responsible for what happened to her?" Chambrun said, still very quiet.

"Homer Woodson, Trudy's father, was president of one of J.W.'s companies," Carlson said. "Woodson Tool and Die. He's been gone for three years—lung cancer. His wife died long before that. Trudy was left alone—well off, but without any family. J.W. took her under his wing, in a kind of way. She had the run of his house. She met Johnny. I guess she'd known him long before that, but they were suddenly close. Knowing Trudy, I'd guess in-bed close. Johnny's attractive, you know, even though he doesn't seem to be overbright. Trudy was very modern. She didn't want marriage, but she stuck to Johnny like glue. She made it clear he was her man."

"Johnny's in serious trouble," Chambrun said, sharper. "I think it's important you get to the point, Carlson."

Carlson reached for the empty glass on the desk. I didn't wait for instructions, but took it over to the sideboard and built him another Jack Daniels on the rocks. I brought it back to him and he took a thirsty swallow of it.

"You must have wondered why J.W. moved into the hotel, Chambrun, when he had a comfortable house on upper Park Avenue," Carlson said.

"He'd bought Johnny an expensive toy," Chambrun said, his eyes narrowed. "I supposed he wanted to be on hand to see how Johnny handled it."

"That's what he wanted you and everybody else to think," Carlson said. "The real reason was far more devious. He is—was—involved in the biggest deal of his life."

"Gamayel's oil deal?"

Carlson nodded. "We're living in strange times, Mr. Chambrun. There's no such thing as secrecy any more. It's a world of leaks. Look at the government, at Grand Juries, at the most secret kind of international diplomacy. Leaks—nothing kept hidden. Only a few people you trust know some fact, and tomorrow your enemies or your competitors have it. This deal with Gamayel's government is so top secret any kind of leak would be fatal. It became apparent that there was leakage from our office, leakage from J.W.'s house. We couldn't plug it up. We couldn't put a finger on it.

So J.W., having bought the hotel, found an excuse to move here—putting Johnny in charge. It removed J.W. from his household staff, his office staff. Whoever was betraying him no longer had access to what he was doing."

"Yet his room was bugged. Johnny's office and his room were bugged," Chambrun said.

"God help us," Carlson said. He took another swallow of his drink. His eyes were red with exhaustion. "He thought he was safe here—safe from eavesdropping or spying. Gamayel was here in the hotel, contact with him easy. Emory Clarke was here to advise him. And then—then there was Trudy."

"I don't follow," Chambrun said.

"It was my suggestion, and I'll never forgive myself for it," Carlson said.

"What suggestion?"

"Who would ever spot Trudy as a spy?" Carlson said. "She was, apparently, just a sex-crazy kid with her number one man now located in the hotel—Johnny. No one would ever pay any attention to her, except as an exciting doll. Nobody would dream she was in J.W.'s confidence. But she took on the job—took it on eagerly. She watched all the comings and goings; she reported to us two or three times a day. Even Johnny didn't know what she was up to. She thought it was fun, exciting. She was Mata Hari—in a mini skirt!" Carlson choked on his drink. "But shrewd and sharp-eyed."

"What had she learned? Anything important?"

"She was in my office, reporting, when we got word of J.W.'s death. She felt she had failed somehow. She said there was someone she suspected and she was going to 'Nail him to the cross.' Those were her words. I urged her to back off. It was out of her hands now. She just laughed at me. And now—now I'll live with the sight of her in that tub forever. I should have stopped her. I didn't.''

"She struck me as a girl who made her own decisions," Chambrun said. "She didn't tell you who this man was she was going to 'nail to the cross'?"

Carlson shook his head. "We spent most of our time trying to guess who was responsible for leaks. We'd guessed everyone from the top down. I asked her—begged her to tell me who she suspected. 'I'm through playing guessing games,' she told me. 'When I'm sure, I'll tell you.'"

Chambrun took time to light one of his flat Egyptian cigarettes. He lit it, took a deep drag on it, and let the smoke out in a pale blue cloud. "So Johnny may have been kidnapped to keep her silent," he said, more to himself than Carlson. "She was designated to deliver the money so that they'd have the opportunity to warn her off. But somebody couldn't wait. She'd gone one step too far, one step closer to exposing someone, and they couldn't wait to warn her off."

Carlson looked up. "And Johnny?" he asked.

"The ransom—if we're guessing right—was just to make it look like a genuine kidnapping. Now that they know Trudy is dead—" Chambrun's eyes were narrowed slits.

"They won't risk a contact? They don't need the money?" Carlson's voice shook. "They'll just—?"

"Remove him from the scene, if they hadn't done so already. Trudy was the key to this. She would deliver the money, unprotected by us or the cops. Standard kidnapping routine. But they wanted her, not money—to silence her one way or another. It turned out they couldn't wait. She was too close."

"So what do we do about Johnny?" Carlson asked.

"We keep this line open—and hope that we're wrong about what they've done to him," Chambrun said.

One of the phones on Chambrun's desk blinked, not the private line. He picked up the phone and I knew he was listening to Ruysdale on the line. "Five minutes," he said finally, and put down the phone.

He faced Carlson, and he was suddenly quite businesslike. "You need to get some rest, and try to get it out of your mind that you're responsible," he said. "I'll have Miss Ruysdale take you up to my penthouse. Get some sleep. She'll provide you with some sleeping pills if you need them. If there is a call, we'll wake you at once."

"I should go back to the office," Carlson said vaguely. "They'll be working there all night."

"You're needed here—in case there should be a call," Chambrun said. "Please do what I ask."

Carlson pulled himself up out of his chair and Chambrun took him out to Ruysdale. When he came back, he took over at his own desk. He handed me Carlson's glass, which I took back to the sideboard.

"One of our mystery men is about to pay us a call," he said. "Mr. James Olin is on his way up from the lobby. Give Hardy a call, will you? I think he should be here for this.''

I'VE DONE A LOT OF TALKING about Carlson's state of shock. I have to admit here I was not much better off. Like Carlson, I couldn't shake the picture of Trudy's mutilated body. And while Johnny-baby had been a pain in the neck to me, the thought of him being done in by the same butchers was almost too much. Johnny had screwed up things at the hotel to an incredible degree while he tried to manage it, but he didn't deserve this kind of retribution.

I had a punishing need to get out of this whirlpool for a while. I thought I needed to get nicely, quietly, blind drunk and sleep it off, hopefully blotting out blood-red visions. Mr. James Olin didn't matter to me. He was just someone J. W. Sassoon had arranged a room for in the hotel. He would explain how that had come about and that would be that.

But I knew Chambrun wasn't going to let me go. There was still an outside chance we might hear something from the kidnappers. There might still be errands to run, tabs to be kept on someone. I made myself a rather larger than normal drink at the sideboard, and before I could touch it, Chambrun asked me to wait in the outer office for Mr. James Olin. Ruysdale had gone up to the penthouse with Carlson. I took the drink with me.

The floor maid had described Olin as being tall, sandy-haired, and wearing green-tinted glasses. She hadn't mentioned that the tinted glasses were in gold wire frames. She hadn't mentioned that he moved with the grace and balance of a well-trained athlete. She hadn't mentioned that his mouth was a thin, straight slit that looked as if it had been cut into his face with a razor blade. She hadn't mentioned that he looked like a man I wouldn't care to meet up with in a dark alley.

"I understand the manager wants to see me," Olin said. His voice was level and cold. People come to the Beaumont from all over the world, and I boast that I have a very good ear for speech patterns. When I'm a little high, I'll bet that I can tell what state a man comes from within one border. James Olin's speech was precise, controlled, and I was reminded of a New England schoolmaster I'd hated when I was in prep school.

"Mr. Chambrun wants to see you," I said. I meant it as a rebuke. No one referred to Chambrun as "the manager," even though that's exactly what he was. I led Olin into the private office.

Chambrun was sitting at his desk, sipping a demitasse of his Turkish coffee. No one spoke for a moment and I had the peculiar sensation of watching two opponents sizing each other up.

"Good evening, Mr. Olin," Chambrun said finally.

"The desk clerk said you wanted to see me," Olin said.

"We've been looking for you since early this morning," Chambrun said.

"I've been away from the hotel since early yesterday evening."

"May I ask where?" Chambrun said.

The light from Chambrun's desk lamp glittered against the green lenses. "You may ask, but I don't believe I'm required to tell you," Olin said.

Chambrun's demitasse cup made a little clicking sound as he put it down, rather firmly, in its saucer. "You are aware that J. W. Sassoon is dead?" Chambrun asked.

"I became aware of it late this afternoon," Olin said.

"How did you become aware?"

"I read it in an afternoon newspaper in Washington, D.C.—if that matters," Olin said. The thin slit of a mouth grew even thinner. "Look here, Mr. Chambrun, I think I know why you want to talk to me. J. W. Sassoon reserved my room for me here and he was taking care of my account with the hotel personally. If you are concerned with who is to pay my bill—"

"You paid your own bill with an American Express card," Chambrun said.

"A technicality. Sassoon paid my account with American Express. Since you seem to have been doing a rundown on me, I supposed you would know that."

"You worked for Sassoon?"

"What is it you want of me, Chambrun? I don't think I have to answer your questions. If you question my credit—"

"I think you do have to answer questions, Mr. Olin," a voice said from the doorway. Hardy had come in unannounced. He looked bushed. He was carrying some papers in his hand.

"Lieutenant Hardy, Homicide Division of the New York police department," Chambrun said.

Sandy eyebrows rose behind the green lenses. "Homicide?" Olin said.

"What you didn't read in the newspaper, Mr. Olin, is that J. W. Sassoon was murdered," Hardy said. "We haven't let it out yet. I'm much too tired to play games with you." He looked down at one of the papers he was carrying. "Your fingerprints were found in Sassoon's room, all over his desk. The FBI has reported on those prints." He read from the paper. "'James Olin, age forty-six; former agent of the CIA, nineteen fifty-eight to nineteen sixty-eight, resigned with an excellent record. Went to work late in nineteen sixty-eight for J. W. Sassoon Enterprises. So far as is known, he is still employed by Sassoon. Expert marksman. During his CIA period he worked in Europe, the Middle East, and Russia. Speaks five languages in addition to English fluently—French, German, Italian, Spanish, and Russian.'"

Hardy looked up from the paper. "There is more about your schooling—college, law school, your marriage which ended in divorce. And on and on, Mr. Olin, including a variety of skills in what might be called violent action. Since your prints were found in the room where Sassoon was murdered, you become a prime suspect. You can refuse to answer questions without having your lawyer present, but in that case you will be arrested on suspicion and the questioning can take place at headquarters. Your choice, Mr. Olin."

During this recital there hadn't been the smallest flicker of change on Olin's hard, set face. "I choose to answer—up to a point."

Hardy sat down in a green leather armchair and stretched his legs out in front of him, a tired man. He fumbled in his pocket for that charred briar pipe. He began to fill it from an oilskin pouch. He wasn't a man in a hurry. I had the pleasant feeling that Olin underestimated him.

"According to this report you have been working for J. W. Sassoon for approximately six years," Hardy said.

"That is correct," Olin said. He clipped off his syllables.

"How does it happen that Mr. Carlson, Sassoon's lawyer, never heard of you?" Hardy asked, looking up with mild eyes.

"The nature of my job. I worked undercover for Mr. Sassoon."

"We'll come to the nature of your job in a moment," Hardy said. "But first, who is Mark Zorich?"

"There is no such person," Olin said.

"You mean you don't know who he is?"

"I mean what I said. There is no such person. 'Mark Zorich' is a name, a cover, an identity that was used to convey messages for and from J. W. Sassoon. When anyone in the labyrinth of companies Sassoon controls got a message or an order from 'Mark Zorich,' they knew it was authentic, authorized by Sassoon himself."

"The last message he delivered was to the effect that Sassoon was dead," Hardy said. "That couldn't have been an authentic message from Sassoon."

"Someone used it to make sure the message was believed," Olin said.

"You?"

"No."

Hardy paused to light his pipe. "So now let's get to your fingerprints on Sassoon's desk, Mr. Olin," he said.

Nothing ruffled James Olin's cool. The green lenses were fixed steadily on Hardy. "Sassoon sent for me to come to his room last night. It was just after eight o'clock. When I got there, he was just eating dinner which had been served him by Room Service. He told me he wanted me to go to Washington for him on a special mission. Facts relating to that mission were contained in papers that were spread out on his desk. He asked me to look at those documents while he finished eating. I sat down at the desk, I handled the papers, I could have left dozens of prints there. He'd finished eating by the time I'd gone through the papers. He gave me my instructions and I left. I got a plane for Washington a little after midnight."

"Taking the papers with you?"

"What I took with me was in my head."

"And who did you go to see in Washington?"

"Sorry," Olin said. "That's a question I won't answer."

"You may need an alibi," Hardy said.

"If I do, I'll find one," Olin said.

"There were no papers found in Sassoon's room."

Olin shrugged. "J.W. wouldn't have left them around for the chambermaid to read—or any guests he might have."

"We have reason to think there was a woman with him when he died," Hardy said.

"He enjoyed the company of women."

"In bed?" Hardy asked.

"That kind of thing was far behind him," Olin said.

Hardy changed his tack. "With J. W. Sassoon dead, who are you working for, Mr. Olin?"

"I would suppose Johnny Sassoon—if anyone."

"Did you know that Johnny Sassoon has been kidnapped?" Hardy asked, very casual.

For the first time something happened to that green-tinted mask of Olin's. A nerve twitched high up on his cheek. "I didn't know. Ransom?"

"Half a million," Hardy said. "Only the person who was supposed to deliver it has also been murdered."

That really seemed to jar Olin. "Who?"

"A girl named Trudy Woodson."

"Jesus!" Olin said, showing emotion for the first time.

"You ever hear of a man named Michael Brent?"

The mask was in place again. "Yes."

"He was shot and then mutilated two years ago. You were working for Sassoon then."

"I was. I tried to find Brent's killer for Sassoon without any luck."

"So did I," Hardy said.

"I know," Olin said. "I double-checked on you. There was no trail."

"Same thing happened to Trudy Woodson," Hardy said. "Shot between the eyes, and then butchered."

"I'd like to lay my hands on that sonofabitch," Olin said as calmly as though he was talking about someone who'd sold him a tough steak. "The Brent thing was the only job I ever failed on for J.W."

"It wasn't your job to protect him?" Hardy asked.

"No. At least not in the sense that I think you mean it. I wasn't a bodyguard. I protected him by countering attempts at espionage by his competitors."

"When you left him to go to Washington—if you went to Washington—did you have any reason to think he was in danger?"

"I went to Washington, and I had no reason to expect trouble."

"You know a man named Gamayel?" Hardy asked.

Again the little nerve twitched. "I know who he is. J.W. was trying to deal with him."

"Does Gamayel know you?"

"Not unless my foot has slipped somewhere."

"You were here in the hotel with Sassoon."

"Nobody knew that. I risked going to his room only once—last night. We talked on the phone when we needed to communicate."

"Did you know Sassoon's phone was bugged, monitored?"

That really seemed to floor Olin. For the first time he moved. He lifted a hand toward his left shoulder and then let it drop.

"Not only was the phone bugged, it was a device that would pick up conversations in the room not on the phone. And Johnny's office was rigged with the same kind of device, and Johnny's room where the

Woodson girl was murdered. Any conversation you had with Sassoon last night was heard by someone.''

The fingers of Olin's right hand flexed and unflexed.

Hardy smiled at him. "You're carrying a gun, Mr. Olin," he said.

"I have a permit for it. Care to see it?"

"I think I need your Washington alibi," Hardy said. "And I'll need to check your weapon, just to be sure it isn't the one that killed Trudy Woodson."

"Any time—about the gun," Olin said.

We were interrupted at that moment by the abrupt entrance of Jerry Dodd, the Beaumont's security officer. Jerry was carrying a package wrapped in newspaper. He was about to blurt out something to us, but when he saw Olin, he cut it off.

"Need to talk to you and Hardy," Jerry said to Chambrun.

Hardy seemed to be enjoying himself. "You got your lunch in that package, Jerry? This is James Olin. I suspect he knows as much about this case as we do. Though maybe I did have a surprise or two for him. What's the excitement?"

"If you say so," Jerry said. He walked over to Chambrun's desk, put down his package, and opened it.

In the package was a gray wig—a man's wig—something that looked like a set of dentures, and a small gray mustache.

"One of my boys found this in a trash can outside the fire exit on the twelfth floor, not far from Johnny Sassoon's room," Jerry said.

Olin and I moved in closer to look at it. It wasn't any kid's halloween kit. The wig was beautifully made and obviously very expensive.

"That's a voice changer," Olin said, pointing to what I'd taken for dentures.

"Voice changer?" Chambrun asked.

"You probably read about one in the Ellsberg case," Olin said. "The White House plumbers? The CIA supplied them with one when they were planning to break into Ellsberg's psychiatrist's office. Wear it and it changes your speech patterns. I saw dozens of them when I worked for the CIA. That wig is a beauty."

"Someone on the twelfth floor wanted to change his appearance in a hurry," Hardy said.

"From man-of-distinction to—what?" Chambrun asked.

THREE

IT WAS AFTER ELEVEN O'CLOCK in the evening of The Day. Our first contact with Johnny-baby's kidnappers had been at seven. Our second had been my conversation with the breather in the telephone booth at 59th Street. That had been at exactly eight o'clock. Since then, nothing. Three hours of nothing. Carlson was waiting in Chambrun's penthouse, knocked out by sleeping pills Ruysdale had persuaded him to take. In her office Ruysdale waited for someone to call in on 232-6668. Chambrun, Hardy, and Jerry Dodd were all making inquiries about a distinguished-looking gray-haired man with a neatly trimmed gray military mustache who might have been seen loitering on the twelfth floor or anywhere else in the hotel. Handling this situation was like a juggler keeping an assortment of balls in the air—the Sassoon murder, the Trudy murder, the kidnapping, a dozen lesser leads to be followed up.

But as Chambrun pointed out—was always pointing out—we still had a hotel to run. It was almost certain that with so many obvious policemen in the lobby and circulating in the halls and in the public rooms some of our regular guests must be beginning to sense that there was something far from ordinary in the wind. I was instructed to do my nightly circulating. If I was asked questions, I was to do what I could to reassure. I didn't ask Chambrun how that was to be accomplished. Did I say, "Don't be nervous. Only three people have met with violence in the last twelve hours or so. Nothing to worry about."

I stopped off at my rooms, which are on the same floor as my office and Chambrun's, to freshen up a little. I found myself thinking about James Olin as I got into a clean shirt and an unwrinkled suit. Movies and suspense novels and the revelations of the Watergate case have given us a pretty frightening picture of men who work for government espionage organizations and for unofficial groups like the White House plumbers. I remembered reading the dossier of one agent who had been involved in political assassinations, the torture of civilians in Vietnam, burglaries, break-ins. All in the day's work. Olin seemed to fit that picture to a T. I wondered how much he'd told us was the truth? I wondered if, when he showed surprise, he was surprised at all. I suspected he was a master actor in whatever situation he found himself. One thing I was sure of. The gun he'd taken out of his shoulder holster and handed over to Hardy before that session in Chambrun's office broke up would not prove to be the one that killed Trudy Woodson. Olin would never have let himself be caught with a murder weapon in his possession.

I don't have a police mind. I don't have Chambrun's flair for solving abstruse puzzles. But it seemed to me that there was something we couldn't be certain of; on which side was Olin really playing? He said he had been working for J. W. Sassoon for six years, a trusted operative. If that was true, it was certain that he'd had nothing to do with the murder of J.W. or the kidnapping of J.W.'s son. It was unlikely he'd had anything to do with Trudy's murder, unless he'd found out that Trudy was working on some other team. But in the world of espionage and spying we hear constantly about what is called the "double agent." The cold man with the green glasses could have worked for J. W. Sassoon for six years while he was, at the same time, taking pay from Sassoon's enemies. The double agent plays both sides of the street and then, in a crisis moment, acts for the highest bidder, for the side that offers him the best future. Olin struck me as a man who would act, without loyalties or conscience, only for his own advantage. I wondered if Chambrun and Hardy had read him that way, too.

When I'd finished dressing, my first stop was the Trapeze Bar. The Trapeze is quite literally suspended in space over the foyer to the Grand Ballroom. The walls are iron grillwork, and some artist of the Calder school has decorated it with a collection of mobiles of circus performers operating on trapezes. The faint circulation of air from a conditioner keeps those little figures in constant motion.

Early curtains at the Broadway theaters mean that by eleven people are already out, and the Trapeze is one of the more popular nightcap places. Of course if you want more entertainment, you go to the Blue Lagoon downstairs where there are music, dancing, and performers. Customers in the Trapeze are usually on the elegant side—quite a lot of dinner jackets and gals wearing long skirts and jewelry that made you wonder where all the money came from. From people connected with the world of giant finance, I told myself; in climates created by people like the late J. W. Sassoon.

I stood in the entrance looking around for people who needed "reassuring." I knew quite a few of the customers and I was nodded at and waved at, but no one seemed frantically in need of being calmed. I was about to turn away when Mr. Del Greco, captain in the Trapeze, joined me.

"I hear things," he said.

"So put cotton in your ears," I said.

"It'll all blow with the morning news," Del Greco said. "Leaks all over the place."

"National pastime," I said.

"There's a gentleman over there at a corner table who wants to talk to you," Del Greco said.

I hadn't noticed Mr. Gamayel in my first survey of the room. He was sitting in the farthest corner, partially screened from view by a party of six sitting directly in front of him. When he caught my eye, he beckoned to me urgently.

I eased my way between tables and joined him. He was wearing an expensively tailored dinner jacket with matching batik cummerbund and tie. A handkerchief of the same colorful material peeped out of his breast pocket.

"I'm grateful to you for joining me, Mr. Haskell," he said.

A waiter was at my elbow almost before I could get seated. Service in the Trapeze is rather special. "Tell Eddie a double usual," I told the waiter. Eddie is the head bartender.

Gamayel's white smile looked pasted on his face. "It has been a black day and night," he said.

I wondered how much he knew. "We've had our troubles," I said.

"Do not play games with me, Mr. Haskell," he said. "The hotel is crawling with spies."

I tried to keep it light. "We're going to recommend to the Police Commissioner that his plainclothes men go to a better tailor," I said.

"I'm not talking about the police," Gamayel said. "Don't look up at once, but directly across the room from you is a dark-haired man wearing a white dinner jacket. He is a member of the Egyptian secret police. His real name is Cecil Treadway, an Englishman, but he works for hire. His hands are bloody."

I couldn't keep from looking up and found myself the object of study by a pair of bright black eyes belonging to the man in the white dinner jacket. I would have spotted him for high society, maybe a member of the international polo set. His mahogany tan suggested outdoor sports. He didn't look away and I was the one who broke off the exchange.

"How do you mean his 'hands are bloody'?" I asked.

The tip of Gamayel's tongue appeared to moisten his lips. "He was a professional assassin for Nasser," he said. "He still works for the Egyptian inner circle. I should not be telling you this, but I must." A little shudder shook his whole body. "It is just possible I may not live out the night, Mr. Haskell."

That jolted me. Melodrama was this little man's dish, but he managed to make it sound believable. He was really scared.

"Why shouldn't you live out the night?" I asked him. I was grateful for the double Jack Daniels the waiter brought.

"I tried to tell you earlier that I came here to attempt to negotiate a deal," Gamayel said. "Treadway's job, obviously, is to stop me. He doesn't know whether I got to Sassoon or not before Sassoon was killed."

"Sassoon died of a heart attack," I said.

Gamayel shook his head. "We are not all children, Mr. Haskell. Treadway will approach me sooner or later and demand the documents I gave to Sassoon. When I cannot produce them, he will assume I made the deal and he will eliminate me."

"So get yourself protection," I said. "The police will protect you."

"For how long? A few days, a few weeks? Treadway will be patient."

"What good will it do him to kill you if you haven't got the documents?" I asked.

"It will be a lesson to other people who may be working against him," Gamayel said. "And Treadway is not the only one. Earlier tonight I saw a man in the lobby I'm certain is a secret agent for the Israelis. They, too, want what I was carrying and what was stolen from Sassoon's room. And there is a killer who works for Sassoon who may think I double-crossed J.W. I am a target. I am caught in a crossfire. I doubt I will see the light of another morning."

"Who is the man who worked for Sassoon?" I asked.

"I do not know his name," Gamayel said. "It could be Zorich, it could be something else."

"A tall, sandy-haired man who wears green-tinted glasses?"

Gamayel's eyes widened. "He is the one."

"And why are you telling me all this, Mr. Gamayel?"

He made a flamboyant little gesture of despair. "I am not afraid to die, Mr. Haskell. But I am human. I would like the man who kills me to pay a price for it."

"But why me—what do you think I can do for you?"

"The police would listen to me and write me off as some kind of paranoid," Gamayel said. "My own government cannot protect me. They cannot own me. They cannot admit I was here to make a deal with Sassoon. I am alone. But I have told you this because I think there is something a little inhuman about you and your Mr. Chambrun."

I think my jaw dropped open. "Inhuman? What the hell are you talking about?"

For the first time he smiled—a sort of thin, conspiratorial smile. "I don't think you or Mr. Chambrun would care two figs whether I died or not. But I do think you would care *where* I die. I think Mr. Chambrun would do anything in his power to prevent there being another murder in his beloved hotel. As I have no intention of leaving your hotel as long as my documents may be found here, and since almost certainly someone will attempt to kill me before the night is out, I assume it would be to Mr. Chambrun's interest—and yours—to see to it that nothing happens to me while I am a guest here.''

The little sonofabitch was right, of course. Chambrun would do anything in his power to put a stop to any more violence in the Beaumont. I only half believed him, you understand. His story was so far out! For certain, however, it would have to be Chambrun who passed judgment on it.

''Finish your drink and we'll go talk to Chambrun,'' I said.

I swallowed the balance of my Jack Daniels and stood up. I couldn't help looking at Cecil Treadway. The Englishman gave me a broad, almost sympathetic grin, as though he knew what I'd been listening to and knew that Gamayel had put me in a bind. That smile almost made a believer of me.

Gamayel and I walked down the circular staircase to the lobby. The little Iraqi managed to walk just behind me, as if he expected any attack that might come would be frontal. My last glimpse of Cecil Treadway had caught him in the act of ordering another drink from the waiter. He wasn't in a hurry—if he actually had any interest in Gamayel.

I stopped at the front desk and asked Karl Nevers if Treadway was registered. He was. I asked for his card so that Chambrun could look at it. As Gamayel and I headed for an elevator, I glanced at the card. Cecil Treadway's home base was London, England. A-1 credit rating, his bank Lloyd's of London. He had stayed at the Beaumont twice before, once five years ago, once two years ago. There was nothing else on the card to indicate any eccentricities that bore watching. He had been a model guest on his previous visits.

Miss Ruysdale was standing guard in the outer office. It had been a long day for her, but she looked completely fresh, untroubled, the ultimate in late-thirties glamor. She smiled at Gamayel as though he was an old and affectionately regarded friend, and then she shut the door on him.

Chambrun had been asking for me. He was occupied at the moment with other people. She thought it would be quite some time before he could see Mr. Gamayel.

Gamayel blotted at his face with the batik handkerchief. Perhaps if Miss Ruysdale were to tell Chambrun that it was a matter of life and death—?

"We've been dealing with life-and-death matters all day, Mr. Gamayel," she said. "I'm afraid you'll have to wait your turn."

He looked at me, his eyes wide. "I have been staying in public places because an attack seemed less likely if I was surrounded by people. But I am exhausted from watching, waiting!"

Miss Ruysdale looked at me. "Your apartment?" she suggested.

As I've said, my apartment is just down the hall. I took Gamayel there, making quite certain that there was no one in the hall watching us.

"There's liquor. You can make yourself coffee," I told him. "There's a double lock and chain on the door. Don't let anyone in except me. As soon as Chambrun's free, I'll come and get you."

I swear he was really afraid, and before he'd let me go he insisted on covering every inch of the apartment—in case someone might be hiding there, for God's sake. In the end he was satisfied and when I stepped out into the hall, I heard both locks snap to and the chain being hooked in place.

Back in the outer office Ruysdale told me that Valerie Brent and Emory Clarke were in with the boss.

"I'm surprised at you, Mark," Ruysdale said, smiling at me. "Is she that attractive? Of course I see her with the supercritical female eye."

I was going to be given the business for the rest of time for having forewarned Valerie.

It looked like a pleasant social evening in Chambrun's office. He sat at his desk with the inevitable Turkish coffee. Valerie and Clarke were in comfortable leather armchairs, each with a drink.

Chambrun raised his hooded eyes to me. "Ruysdale informs me that Gamayel is in some kind of a sweat," he said.

"He's on ice in my apartment," I said. "He doesn't expect to live out the night, he says. There's an Englishman named Treadway who is an assassin for the Egyptian government. There's an undercover agent for the Israelis. There's whoever stole his documents. He hopes you will protect him because you won't want someone else killed in your hotel."

"He's quite right," Chambrun said.

"You don't take him seriously?" Clarke asked.

"He lives in a world of melodrama," I said. "He's scared, but how serious his trouble is, I doubt a little." Valerie was looking at me and her lovely eyes were saying "Thank you," and I was starting to feel giddy again. I put Treadway's registration card down on Chambrun's desk. He looked at it, scowling.

"Cecil Treadway, London-based," he said. "You don't happen to know him do you, Mrs. Brent?"

Valerie shook her head, frowning slightly.

"He's dark, handsome, athletic-looking," I said. "Perfectly tailored. Gamayel pointed him out to me in the Trapeze."

"A coincidence of sorts," Chambrun said. He looked straight at Valerie. "He has stayed with us twice before. Once five years ago. That's when you and your husband stayed with us, Mrs. Brent. Once two years ago. That's when your husband was killed."

Clarke was spilling ashes down his front as usual. "I've heard some things about Treadway," he said. "As a matter of fact I recognized him in the lobby the other day. There are two areas in which I'm supposed to be something of a political expert: South America and the Middle East. Those worlds are full of people working for different power groups, some openly, some under cover, some both ways. Treadway was living in Cairo the last time I spent any time out there. He was very popular with the international set. The extra man for dinner parties par excellence. There were rumors about him—what wives he had seduced, how much money he'd won at cards from some rich innocent. But mostly what I heard was that he was a dangerous man to cross. It was hinted he had something to do with some rather gruesome killings. No proof, of course. But it was the talk. If he really is after Gamayel, the little man has a right to be frightened."

"I gather, from what you told us earlier," Chambrun said, "that the stakes in the game Gamayel is playing are high."

"High. Extra high," Clarke said.

"Just exactly what is the game?" Chambrun asked. "Someone involved in it is turning my world here into a slaughterhouse. They must be stopped."

Clarke held his glass up, studying the amber liquid in it against the light from the windows. "I know a thing or two about you, Mr. Chambrun," he said, smiling that amiable smile of his. "Thirty years ago you were a super-hero, fighting in the French Resistance movement against the Nazis."

"That is ancient history and beside the point," Chambrun said. He occasionally mentioned what he called "the dark days" of the Resistance, but even after all this time I could sense that the memory caused him pain.

"I mention it only because the political ramifications of any underground movement are so tremendously varied; you must be aware of that from that past time. You hear a thousand rumors, all coming from what the press calls 'reliable sources.' Not a tenth of them are true."

"How much more reliable than you could any source be?" Chambrun said. He sounded sharp. "You told us that you consulted with J. W. Sassoon in the last day or two. What is the game? What, precisely, are the stakes?"

"You have only to wander around in the corridors of that United Nations to hear all that I've heard, know all that I know," Clarke said. He lit a fresh cigarette from the stub of the one he was smoking. "The Middle East is oil," he said. "For a hundred years or more the oil fields out there have been leased and operated by Western powers—first Great Britain and then the United States. The rulers of those strange Arab countries have grown fat and rich on Western money—the British pound and the American dollar."

"Do I need a lesson in economics?" Chambrun asked. I was surprised at his impatience, the angry glitter in his hidden eyes.

Clarke gave him a paternal smile. "Of course not. It is a sketchy background, perhaps necessary for you to understand the present turmoil," he said. "Demands for oil are increasing beyond belief—oil for tanks, and gun carriers and planes, and armored vehicles. Oil for war and preparedness against war. Then there are millions of automobiles, increasing by the hundreds of thousands almost annually. Oil has replaced coal in industry. Every man living in a nontropical climate heats his home with oil, uses oil to mow his lawns, for God's sake. There was a time when the United States' own oil production was enough for its needs. No more. But no cause for worry, you understand. The United States had control of vast amounts of oil around the world. That control depended on two things, Mr. Chambrun. Those two things were contracts written on pieces of paper and the force of arms to keep those contracts valid. So things have changed."

"Exactly how?" Chambrun asked.

"The rulers of these countries are still fat and rich, but they now see ways of getting even fatter and

richer—and also much more powerful. They have
been fed with the virus of revolution. They have been
led to believe they can seize control of their oil supplies and to hell with the contracts. They can triple
their wealth by tripling the price they will sell for. And
who will buy at these inflated prices? The West desperately needs the oil, but now the Communist world
needs it equally badly. The threat of military power to
enforce old contracts is not so much of a threat as it
once was. The big powers are reluctant to use force,
for fear some madman might press a button that
would destroy the whole world. So it becomes a matter of wheeling and dealing. The little kings and the
little tyrants hold the whip hand. If they sell to us, the
Communists will moan, and groan, and threaten but
they will not actually move in force against us. If they
sell to the Communists, we will moan and groan but
we will not strike. So it comes down to what you might
call grassroots free enterprise. The highest bidder will
get it. And with what does he bid? Money? Some, of
course, but also guns and planes so that the little kings
and tyrants can protect themselves from each other
and also from Israel, which poses a constant threat. It
is a seller's market, Mr. Chambrun.''

"J. W. Sassoon was a buyer, right?" Chambrun
asked.

"Oh, yes, very much so. He was a man with more
money than you can dream of. One of the sources of
his wealth was a vast production of war material. He
was a man who could bid against government.''

"And he needed your advice," Chambrun said.

"My field is politics," Clarke said. "It's called diplomacy in the upper echelons. Which brings me to your Mr. Gamayel."

"At last," Chambrun said.

Clarke put down his empty glass. "Mr. Gamayel is a part of a new world, Mr. Chambrun. He has told you, I gather, that he represents his government; that he was discussing a deal with Sassoon for his government. The missing documents?" Clarke laughed. "Like most of the business and political world today, Mr. Gamayel is playing two sides of the street. He represents his government at the United Nations, but in this projected deal with J. W. Sassoon he represents other interests. Mr. Gamayel wants to be an important man on a winning team. There is a group in his country ready to seize power from the present government. This countergroup is trying to deal, before the fact, with potential buyers of the country's oil. If they can show that they are in business before they strike, a lot of people will turn coats for them. They preferred to deal with a private buyer, like Sassoon, than with governments—like Washington or Moscow. Too many people get a piece of the pie when you deal with governments."

"Sassoon asked for your advice," Chambrun said.

"He asked for my opinion. Could Gamayel's countergroup actually make it? Could they seize the power?"

"And you told him?"

"That if they could make a deal with him in advance—or a deal with someone of equal power—they could make it. So you can see why Mr. Gamayel is so

concerned about his missing documents and why he
has a right to be afraid.''

"Not quite," Chambrun said.

"Because those documents will reveal not just a financial arrangement with J. W. Sassoon, but an up-
coming coup. Probably names, dates, and the like. In
the hands of the present government this information
might make it possible for them to abort the coup before it can take place. Mr. Gamayel stands to be killed
by one side for having been a traitor, and by the other
for having been criminally careless and exposing their
plans before they can set them in motion. Whichever
side gets to him first is very likely to polish off Mr.
Gamayel.''

"And for which side might a man like Treadway be
working?"

Clarke shrugged. "Either side. He works for money.
It can't make very much difference to Gamayel, however, since both sides will be out to get him.''

"His danger is real, then?''

"I would say very real.''

Chambrun picked up one of his phones and asked
the switchboard to locate Jerry Dodd and have him
report. "He'll need more than a locked door to protect him," Chambrun said. He looked at Valerie, who
had sat, motionless, through Clarke's exposition. "I
regret going into a painful past with you, Mrs. Brent,
but I'm afraid I must. Five years ago you and your
husband stayed with us here in the Beaumont. Do you
remember what he was working on then—nineteen
sixty-eight?''

"Michael came over here to write some articles on the Presidential campaigns for a British magazine," she said.

"Nothing connected with the Middle East?"

She hesitated. "Michael had been very concerned with the Arab-Israeli confrontation. He did a book on the six-day war, you know."

"So Treadway might have had an interest in him then?"

"I can't think what," Valerie said. "If he was working for one of the countries out there, I suppose—"

"The next time you came here was two years ago," Chambrun said, his face expressionless. "Your husband was working on a biography of J. W. Sassoon."

"Not so much a biography of Sassoon as of Sassoon's empire," Valerie said.

"Sassoon had been involved in Middle East oil for twenty-five years. That must have been part of your husband's story."

Valerie looked down at her hands, which were locked together in her lap. "Very much a part of it. Michael told me, many times, that J. W. Sassoon was one of the original robber barons. 'I'm going to write things in this book he isn't going to like,' Michael told me."

"Lieutenant Hardy tells me you thought they quarreled over this material."

"They did. Mr. Sassoon was in a rage about it, but Michael intended to go right ahead—was going ahead—"

"That's why you thought Sassoon might be responsible for your husband's death? Killed him and burned his manuscript?"

"Yes," Valerie said. It was a whisper.

"And yet the mysterious Mr. Treadway is on the scene once more. Is it possible there were things in the manuscript that other interests might have objected to?"

"I suppose so," Valerie said. "Michael wrote the truth as he found it."

Chambrun looked at Clarke. "Does it seem likely to you that Treadway could have been working for J.W.? He had his own man for rough stuff—James Olin."

"Treadway could have been working for anyone," Clarke said. "A job at a time. He has never had any allegiances, any flag, any loyalties."

"One more question about this whole intrigue, Mr. Clarke. Involved are the present government of Mr. Gamayel's country and the countergroup planning a coup. There could be a third group involved, couldn't there? A group that could use Mr. Gamayel's documents to blackmail the countergroup, or buy favors from the present government?"

Clarke nodded, his smile faded. "Whoever has those documents has the power to change history," he said. "You see, if a third person or group—"

He never finished, because Chambrun's office was shaken by something that sounded like an enormous explosion. Chambrun was on his feet in a second, headed for the door. There have been endless bomb scares over the last few years.

Miss Ruysdale, looking as nearly rattled as I've ever seen her, met Chambrun at the door.

"It seems to be on this floor," she said.

We went through her office and out into the hall. The air was thick with what looked like plaster dust to me. It was thickest down the hall near my office, my apartment. We were just approaching the center of it, choking on the dust, when Jerry Dodd, our security officer, came racing up the stairs from the lobby.

"Thank God you're all right, boss," he said to Chambrun. "When I heard it, I thought it was in your office."

We'd reached the door to my apartment by then—only there wasn't any door. It had been blown off its hinges. Jerry tried to stop Chambrun, but Chambrun was ahead of all of us into my rooms. It was almost impossible to breathe. The dust was thick and there was the acrid smell of some kind of gunpowder or explosive. The two locks and the chain on my door had not protected Mr. Gamayel.

But Mr. Gamayel was nowhere in the apartment. Some china had been smashed by the explosion, a painting knocked off the far wall, a chair overturned. Chambrun quickly checked the kitchen, the bathroom, the bedroom. No Gamayel.

There were little tongues of flame around the door frame and I found myself pushed aside by Jerry Dodd, who had dug up a fire extinguisher. It was still like looking at a pea soup London fog, everyone coughing and choking. Someone took me by the arm and turned me around. I found myself looking down into Valerie Brent's wide, hazel eyes.

"Please help me, Mark," she whispered. "For God's sake, help me!"

For a stupid moment I thought she was hurt. I reached out for her and I could feel her body trembling.

"Come to my room when you can," she said.

Then Clarke loomed up out of the fog and put a protective arm around her shoulders. "It looks as if we were a little late to help Gamayel," he said. He looked down at Valerie. "Let me get you out of here, Val. We're just in the way."

He took her off, headed for the staircase leading down to the lobby. She didn't look back at me.

PART THREE

ONE

CHAMBRUN WAS QUICKER to put the scene into per-
spective than anyone else. I heard him giving orders to
Jerry Dodd.

"You'll put B Plan into operation at once, Jerry."

"Right."

"And nobody is to leave this hotel, not even
through a rat hole, without an okay. Don't take any
'diplomatic immunity' crap from anybody."

When Chambrun uses that kind of language, his
anger has reached the explosion point. A couple of
Jerry's men and a couple of cops came crowding
through my charred doorway.

"Get moving, man!" Chambrun said to Jerry.
"There's nothing to do here but make sure the fire's
out!" He took me by the arm and literally dragged me
out into the hall. Miss Ruysdale was hovering there.
"Get back to the office, Ruysdale!" he ordered her.
"We're putting B Plan into operation."

We were all three of us gasping for breath when we
got back into his air-conditioned suite of offices.
B Plan was a method for dealing with bomb threats.
They'd been a dime a dozen a while back. Hotels,
banks, even Grand Central Station had been a target
for that kind of terror tactic. The problem was how to
deal quickly with the situation when some crackpot
called in to tell us there was a bomb planted some-

where in the Beaumont. The hotel was thirty stories
high, plus the three penthouses on the roof, plus three
basements and subbasements below the lobby floor,
over nine hundred private and public rooms, including the shops in the lobby area. Figuring a minimum
of ten minutes to search a room thoroughly, you were
talking about a hundred and fifty man-hours of
work—like six days! It became a simple matter of lo-
gistics. Turn fifteen people loose on each floor simul-
taneously and you could pretty well cover the whole
place in half an hour. This meant using practically
every employee on duty in the hotel at any given
time—maids, housekeepers, cleaning crews, bell-
hops, doormen, waiters, bartenders, office person-
nel, and, of course, the security staff. Everyone had a
specific assignment. If guests were not in their rooms,
passkeys were used. If guests were reluctant to admit
searchers—and it wasn't unlikely that we might barge
in on situations where the wrong people were in the
wrong beds—we were instructed to be firm, as blind
to indiscretion as possible. If that didn't work, then
Chambrun himself was called on to handle the situation.

"You think there may be more bombings?" Miss
Ruysdale asked Chambrun.

"No. But I want the bomber. I want Olin and
Treadway. I want Gamayel."

"If he's still alive," I said. The force of the explosion at my door must, I thought, have knocked Gamayel cold.

"You think someone's carrying him around the hotel dead or unconscious?" Chambrun asked. "He wasn't in the room when that door was blown open."

"He was there!" I said. "I heard him lock himself in. Two locks and the chain."

"So he let himself out," Chambrun said. "We were down the hall thirty or forty seconds after the explosion. No one had time to drag a body out of there and get away with it."

"He was too scared to leave the rooms," I said.

"More scared of something else, maybe," Chambrun said. He turned to Ruysdale. "Find out if Gamayel made a call from Mark's rooms, or if he received a call."

Chambrun went to his phones and called Karl Nevers at the front desk. No one was to leave the hotel without an okay. "I know it could start a riot," Chambrun said. "I want Treadway, Olin, and Gamayel. I want any strangers that you don't know or who can't be vouched for by people we trust. Any of the regulars who want out can go, but I want a record of who's allowed to leave."

Miss Ruysdale came back from her office. "They don't keep any kind of record of Mark's out-calls," she said, "unless, of course, they're long distance. But in-calls are a little different. The operator holds on until the phone is answered. That's a routine on all in-calls through the switchboard. If there's no answer, there may be a message. There was a call in about forty minutes ago. The operator remembers because it wasn't Mark who answered. A man with a slight accent, she says. But when the connection was made, she cut out.''

"Gamayel has an accent," I said.

"He does, and he went out after he got the call," Chambrun said.

"He was too scared to go out," I insisted.

"Not if someone told him where he could find his precious documents," Chambrun said. "Two sides are after him. One of them tried to bomb him out, the other suckered him out with a phone call. He'd have been safer facing the bomb, I think."

It was then that I told Chambrun about Valerie Brent's plea for help. I wasn't going to play the Lone Ranger a second time. Phones were blinking on Chambrun's desk.

"Maybe you should find out what it is," he said. He gave me an odd look. "If it turns out to be your sexual prowess that's needed, be good enough to put it off until sometime when I don't require your services."

It had only been a few minutes since the word had gone out, but already people were reporting to their posts in accordance with B Plan. Cops and technicians were swarming around and in my apartment, but down the hall I saw people were already in my office searching for a bomb Chambrun didn't expect them to find. We were going to be covered from top to bottom before midnight. It was going to be an embarrassing night for the sexual adventurers.

I got an elevator to the eighth floor. A crew consisting of maids, the housekeeper, members of the cleaning crew, room service waiters, and a couple of Jerry's men were already knocking on doors up and down the corridor. I gathered some of the situations were pretty sticky, but the word "bomb" worked wonders with most of them.

A maid was knocking at Valerie's door.

"No one home, I guess," she said.

"Then use your passkey," I said.

I felt a moment of panic as the maid fumbled with her key and finally got the door open. Valerie had asked me to come when I could. I had expected her to be there.

The room was just as the maids are trained to leave things in the evening—a light burning on the bedside table, the bed turned down. The maid had been trained how to make her search, and I stood in the center of the room looking around vaguely. So help me, I didn't want to go into the bathroom. I had been in Trudy Woodson's. The maid went straight there, however, and there were no cries of horror from her. I was aware of Valerie's presence, a faint, personalized perfume. The maid opened the closet door and I saw her clothes hanging there. She went for bright colors. I knew I wanted to find her very badly.

It occurred to me that she and Clarke might have stopped in one of the main floor bars for a drink. It would be natural enough. They must have been pretty well shaken up by the bombing.

I found Clarke, but he was alone. He was nursing a highball in the Spartan Bar, last bastion of chauvinist male pigs. No women allowed in the Spartan. Johnnybaby had meant to break that down with his topless cigarette girls. The Spartan is always quiet. Several old-timers were playing chess and backgammon in a far end of the room. I joined Clarke.

"I welcome company," he said. "I was just getting ready to turn in when an army descended on my room, looking for bombs, they said. I decided on a quiet drink. Does Chambrun really expect more explosions?"

"He's using a planned system—really trying to find Treadway, Olin, and Gamayel," I said.

"I trust he isn't locking the barn door too late," Clarke said.

A waiter brought me a double Jack Daniels on the rocks, an automatic. I realized I'd poured down quite a little alcohol in the last twelve hours. It might as well have been water.

"I was looking for Val to make sure she's all right," I said. "She seemed a little stunned by what's been happening."

He looked at me, eyes twinkling. "I wish I was your age," he said. "That's a one-in-a-million woman, but you'd have to be all man to handle her." He rattled the ice in his glass. "I've unfortunately reached that age when my supply can't meet the demand."

"You don't look it," I said.

"Flattery'll get you noplace," he said. His face clouded. "The butchery of that Woodson child has brought Val's own tragedy back to her all too vividly. Do you think your Lieutenant Hardy is satisfied with her account of how her package of underthings was stolen?"

"Why not?" I said. "But we'd all like to know how they turned up in Sassoon's room."

"Obvious frame-up," Clarke said, scowling. "They hoped you'd believe J.W. died from an overindulgence in sexual exercise. J.W. would never have gone for a call girl, but no one could resist Val if she made herself available."

"These bastards are so elaborate!" I said.

"It's an elaborate game with an elaborate pattern," Clarke said. "When you get a glimpse of the behind-the-scenes manipulations of governments, of business conglomerates, it's dumbfounding. 'Morality' and 'ethics' are just words used in public to satisfy an unsophisticated public. When you get down to bedrock, there's only one thing that matters. Checkmate the enemy and collect the reward for winning. Ways and means are only a matter of concern to naive idiots." As he spoke, a bitterness came into his voice I hadn't heard there before.

"I have a hunch they may be in for a surprise," I said.

"Oh?" Clarke looked at me, his craggy eyebrows raised.

"When Chambrun is driven to playing it rough, they may be surprised at just how rough he can be," I said.

Clarke sighed and lit a cigarette. "Interesting man, your Mr. Chambrun," he said. "You expect a hotel manager to be a sort of expert traffic cop—keeping things running efficiently and smoothly. I've had reason once or twice in the past—when I've been involved with the State Department—to inquire about him. Some very important foreign dignitaries make the Beaumont their 'home-away-from-home.' I know, from personal experience, that Chambrun has been asked to handle some very delicate and top-secret negotiations for State. As a very young man he was a tiger in the struggle against the Nazis occupying Paris. But that was long ago, Mark. The lines were clearly drawn. No doubt about who were the good guys and who the bad guys. Today's ball game is played by entirely different rules. Definitions aren't so clear. The good guys and the bad guys all look alike. Today there are only winners and losers. Your best friend, your own father, may step on your neck and wipe you out tomorrow if you stand in the way of his winning." Cigarette ash dribbled down on his necktie. The bitterness in his voice had a sharper edge. "As I said, thirty years ago your man was a tiger, but I wonder if his teeth are sharp enough this much later."

"I think they may be," I said. "I wouldn't want him to test them out on me."

Clarke took a deep drag on his cigarette and watched the smoke curl upward as he exhaled. "Tell your Mr. Chambrun something for me," he said. "Something I suspect he already knows. I wouldn't take a step near the center of this mess. I care too much for my own hide. If he comes even close to the inner circle of this particular intrigue, they'll wipe him out—like that! He'll never know what happened. Tell him for me I'm afraid he can't learn to play this newfangled ball game well enough to win. He may be tough, but at bottom he's a decent man. That decency will always make him hesitate a second too long when the showdown comes. I could give you a long list of decent and patriotic men who have tried to match their toughness and dedication against today's amoral power boys. Most of them are dead. A few of them live—crippled as far as productive lives are concerned—wishing they were dead." Clarke gave a little mirthless laugh. "Believe me, I know when to back away. Tell Chambrun to let the police do the hunting. They'll muddle out of it in some way. Tell Chambrun for me that if he insists on trying to dig deeper, I think he'll be pronouncing his own death sentence."

When he'd started to talk, I thought Clarke was just theorizing. When he came to the end of it, I had the uncomfortable feeling that he meant his warning to be very real.

"You're serious," I said. "You really want me to tell Chambrun what you've said."

"I've never been more serious in my life," he said. "What do you know about me, Mark?"

"A distinguished statesman," I said. "A man who knows certain parts of the world better than most other men. A trusted servant of our government."

Again that short, mirthless laugh. "I should designate you to deliver the eulogy at my funeral," he said. "I am more nearly like your Mr. Chambrun than you know. Somewhere inside me there has always been that spark of decency. I've never been quite able to pay the price to reach the top. The big prize has always been there for the taking if I'd had the guts. If I'd been willing to risk my life to take it. It's too late for Chambrun to try to stop a rockslide or a tornado. It's not within a decent man's power." He put out his cigarette with something like ferocity. "Tell him I never meant anything so sincerely. Now, if you want to check out on Val, you'd better do it. She'll have turned in, I imagine."

"She wasn't in her room a few minutes ago," I said.

He looked at me, his eyebrows raised. "I took her straight there when we left your apartment," he said. "She didn't want to talk or have a drink."

"She isn't there now."

"Perhaps she just wants to pull herself together in private," Clarke said. "Maybe, like me, she left her room when your bomb squad arrived."

"They were just knocking on her door when I got there," I said. "Does she have other friends in the hotel she may have joined?"

"She hasn't mentioned anyone to me," he said. "Of course she has friends in the city. She may have decided to go out."

She'd asked me to come to her room when I could. Her plea to me had been too urgent for me to be comfortable with that suggestion.

I left Clarke, telling him I had to circulate. I tried Valerie's room from a house phone in the lobby on the chance she'd gone back there after I'd left. No answer.

I flagged down Mike Maggio, the night bell captain, who was circulating in the lobby. I knew his assignment was to keep things under control there and to help out the people on the main doors in case someone got obstreperous about leaving. I asked him if he'd seen Valerie.

"Earlier," he said. "She had dinner with old man Clarke. She in some kind of trouble?"

"The way things are going around here, anything unexplained smells like trouble," I said. "She asked me to catch up with her, but she isn't in her room. Keep an eye out for me."

"Will do," he said. His face darkened. "Nothing new on Johnny-baby?" I remembered it was Mike who had first dubbed the Sassoon heir "Johnny-baby."

"Nothing after the first demand for ransom," I said.

"He and the Woodson doll were babes-in-the-woods in this scenario," Mike said. "Johnny-baby sure didn't know how to run a hotel, but he was a decent kid. I'd help him if I knew how." He was the second person to be concerned with decency in the last few minutes. There wasn't much of it around at the moment, that was for sure.

I saw lights blinking on and off in some of the dress shops, the drugstore, the gift and book store that were located off the lobby. The search was in full swing.

I was just starting for the stairway to report to Chambrun when I saw him barging across the lobby to the front desk with Jerry Dodd in tow. I joined them.

"We've located Olin," he told me. "He's in his room, but he refuses to let anyone in." Karl Nevers on the desk handed over a set of passkeys for the fourth-floor rooms. Chambrun and Jerry started for the elevators and I tagged along, telling the boss that I hadn't been able to find Valerie. That didn't seem to concern him very much. On the way up in the elevator, I gave him the gist of Clarke's message.

"I can turn it on or off at will," Chambrun said.

"Turn what on or off?"

"Any basic decency or human sympathy," he said.
"I learned how to do that long ago. Hesitate? Every
ten minutes I remind myself of Trudy Woodson cut to
pieces in that bathroom upstairs. Don't think there'll
be a moment's hesitation if I find myself facing the
bastard who's responsible for that."

We reached the fourth floor and went along the
corridor to the door of James Olin's room. Two of the
fourth-floor search crew were standing there, looking
uncertain.

"Any other trouble on this floor?" Chambrun
asked.

"Nothing, Mr. Chambrun. We didn't find anything, either—or the people you're looking for. Only
this."

Chambrun pounded on the door. "Olin? This is
Pierre Chambrun. Open up."

After a moment the door opened a little, but only
as far as the chain lock would permit. One green lens
looked out at us.

"I've had about enough of this, Chambrun," Olin
said. "Your people say they're looking for a bomb.
You can assure them there isn't one in here. I've
looked."

"I want to talk to you," Chambrun said, "and I'm
coming in."

"And I don't choose to let you," Olin said.

"It'll take me about three minutes to saw through
that chain," Jerry said. "And if you try to jam the

door closed on my foot, friend, I'll take pleasure in smashing your foot when I get inside."

Olin laughed. "So we're going to play rough!" he said. "Well, you're going to have to take your foot out of the door if I'm to unhook this chain."

Chambrun nodded and Jerry stepped back. The door closed, and then opened. Olin faced us, fully dressed. He certainly hadn't been going to bed. The room looked perfectly normal, perfectly neat.

"This is pretty damned highhanded, Chambrun," Olin said.

"Security problems," Chambrun said, his bright black eyes covering the room. "I'm sure my people told you that a bomb blew the door off Mark's apartment on the second floor. This is a routine check of the whole hotel."

"My ass!" Olin said, smiling his thin smile. "You particularly want to talk to me, right? Am I number one or number two on your list? Have you located Treadway? You ought to think of him first, you know."

"We've found you first," Chambrun said.

"Well, I've been thinking about it and I've decided to make it easy for you," Olin said. He moved to the bedside table and took a cigarette from an open pack that was lying there. He snapped a gold lighter into flame. "I want Treadway just as badly as you do," he said. "Not because he killed some people. That's the name of the game. I want him because he stole some documents that belong to J. W. Sassoon Enterprises. They're the people I work for."

"So make it easy for us," Chambrun said.

"I've been in touch with certain contacts of mine," Olin said, "and I've decided to provide you with my Washington alibi. You see, I didn't kill J.W. I didn't kill that girl upstairs. I didn't kidnap Johnny. I was in Washington, or in transit from Washington when all that happened. I believe you know a man in the State Department named George Fentriss. He says he knows you well."

Chambrun's eyes narrowed. "I know him well," he said.

"Call him," Olin said. "He'll tell you that I was with him in Washington from approximately ten o'clock this morning—yesterday morning to be precise—until about eight o'clock in the evening, when he put me on the shuttle flight back to New York. I was either with Fentriss or in the air flying back here when J.W. was killed, when Johnny disappeared, and when the Woodson girl was killed." His thin smile widened. "I have no alibi for your bombing. I was here in the hotel. But you'll have to prove a case against me."

"You have a phone number for Fentriss? Call him," Chambrun said.

Olin picked up the phone and gave the switchboard a Washington number. It was so quiet in the room while we waited I could hear the ticking of the little bedside alarm clock on the table. Then the connection was made.

"Mr. Fentriss?" Olin asked. "James Olin here. I have Mr. Chambrun ready to talk to you." He held out the phone.

"George?" Chambrun asked. "Yes, well, we're up to our necks in trouble here. Olin tells me you can account for him from ten in the morning till eight in the evening." He listened to what the Washington man had to tell him. Olin's green glasses were fixed on him. "I'm not concerned at the moment with why he was there, George. Just that he *was* there. I'm grateful. Thank you." Chambrun put down the phone. "That seems to do it, Olin."

"It hurts my pride to have to prove anything to anyone," Olin said. "But I think we need each other, Chambrun. I want Treadway maybe even more than you do."

"You think Treadway is responsible for this mass shambles?"

Olin shrugged. "Who else?" he said. "J.W. was on the verge of making a deal with the people Gamayel represents. It would have put the people Treadway works for out of business. The documents that are missing reveal an entire conspiracy to overthrow Treadway's crowd. A small army of people named in those documents are likely to be put up against a wall and shot. Naturally those people want the documents before Treadway can deliver them to his people. Gamayel wants them before they reveal him as a double agent—working for both sides. I want them because J. W. Sassoon Enterprises can't afford to be linked with the conspirators in case they lose out. Someone else would be able to make the big deal then. No one would deal with J. W. Sassoon Enterprises if they were known to have been dickering with the conspirators. So it's documents, documents, who's got the documents?"

"And Treadway would resort to murder and kidnapping to get them?" Chambrun asked.

That baleful smile widened. "So would I," Olin said. "But Treadway made it. Now, if he gets away, I'll have blown it. So I'm after your help to find him."

"You said it could be a third party."

"Let's face it," Olin said. "Treadway is one of the top men in the business with electronic gadgets. You tell me there were bugs all over the hotel, installed right under your nose. Treadway is a genius at that kind of thing. He's an expert with explosives. He's a cold-blooded killer. I always believed he killed Michael Brent, but I was never able to pin it on him. The same trademark turns up in the case of the Woodson girl. Two and two."

"But you had thoughts about other people?"

Olin nodded. "Gamayel, always the double agent. He doesn't have the nerve for killing, but Treadway just could be working for him. Treadway will work for anyone if the price is right. I even thought of Mrs. Brent. She's been hysterical on the subject of revenge. I warned J.W. that her apparent change of heart about him was a phony. But killing the girl is out of line for her, and she couldn't change a fuse, let alone install sophisticated electronic listening devices. She hated J.W., but she's not a professional."

"Her newly bought lingerie was found in J.W.'s room," Chambrun said quite casually. "Sex can be a powerful weapon."

Olin laughed. "You know, I thought of that," he said. "It would be a woman's way to kill, wouldn't it? Tempt an old man with a weak heart into bed with her and let him die from the exertion. Mrs. Brent would have been tempting, but J.W. was a realist. He knew the condition of his heart. He didn't want to die just now. He had big irons in the fire.''

"He didn't die from sexual exertion," Chambrun said. "He was smothered with a pillow and there's a nice clear thumbprint on the headboard of the bed. Not yours, Mr. Olin, or the tenor of this conversation would be a little different. But how do you explain Mrs. Brent's lingerie in the room?''

"I was playing with that one when you began banging on my door," Olin said. "You see, before all this went into motion, I was watching Mrs. Brent. I figured she had something cooked up against the old man. I thought she might have an ally. I was keeping her under surveillance. I saw her buy that stuff at Charlene's and bring it back to the hotel. How to figure, after the fact? Well, I told myself, she planned to seduce the old boy, went to his rooms, prepared to go into the 'getting into something comfortable' routine, found him dead, panicked and left her nice new black seduction clothes behind her.''

"But that couldn't be," I said. "The things were stolen from her before she got them back to the hotel!''

The green glasses turned my way. "Stolen?''

I barged on, ignoring the warning look Chambrun gave me. "She stopped in the park on the way home, sat down on a bench watching some children play. Some guy in a loud sports shirt and white buckskin shoes came up behind her, snatched the package, and took off with it. So someone framed her.''

Chambrun's look was withering. "Aren't you for-getting, Mark, that Mr. Olin says he was following Mrs. Brent?"

"Then he must have seen it happen!" I said.

"I can't imagine why she would tell you that," Olin said, "because I can assure you she never stopped in the park, and there was no man in a loud sports shirt and white buckskin shoes there, or anywhere else."

"So you're probably right," Chambrun said. "She planned a seduction, arrived too late, panicked."

He accepted it so readily. I wanted to tell him that nothing on earth would make me believe that Valerie Brent would have allowed herself to be mauled by that monstrous old jellyfish. To kill him? It was nonsense.

I was suddenly aware that all the while we'd been talking, Jerry Dodd had been going over the room pretty carefully. Olin was aware of it too. "No evi-dence that I manufactured a bomb here, Mr. Dodd?"

Jerry didn't answer. He was looking at Chambrun for instructions. Chambrun seemed to be in no hurry.

"It's up to Lieutenant Hardy to deal with two known murders," he said. "We're concerned with preventing any further violence, and, if possible, ne-gotiating for Johnny Sassoon's release. You're a professional, Mr. Olin. You tell us Cecil Treadway is the man we should be after. You tell us he is a cold-blooded killer; you tell us he's an electronics and ex-plosives expert; you tell us he could be working for Gamayel's government, or some third party, not the group that was dickering with Sassoon. So how do you read the evidence, you, a professional? Let's take it step by step. To begin with, your alibi isn't quite as good as it sounds."

"In what way?" Olin asked. I thought they sounded like two chess players discussing the moves of a game they'd already played.

"You told us Sassoon summoned you about dinnertime. He wanted you to look at documents. I take it some of them were the documents that are supposed to be missing?"

"Are missing," Olin said.

"You left your fingerprints all over the desk. Sassoon, served by Room Service, ate his dinner while you were looking at the papers. The room service waiter saw you?"

"Yes."

"Then you say you left Sassoon, carrying information in your head, and made arrangements to go to Washington. Did you leave Sassoon alive?"

Olin smiled. "Not my fingerprint on the headboard, remember? Talk to the room service waiter. He'll tell you I was gone when he came to take away the tray. I hope he'll tell you that J.W. was alive."

"How was Sassoon dressed when you saw him?"

"Trousers, white shirt with no tie, a seersucker robe."

"He was stark naked when the maid found him dead in the morning," Chambrun said. "He must have been stark naked when he was killed. Who would he let into his room when he was naked? The windows in that suite are barred, because it's a straight drop to the street. No way in or out except through the door. In theory no one could come in unless he wanted them in. Why would he receive somebody without any clothes on?"

"There are passkeys," Olin said. He frowned. "We come again, of course, to the possibility of the lady. He might well have gotten undressed after she came."

"So he is smothered with a pillow—maybe by the lady, but from that thumbprint I'd guess a rather large man. The papers are stolen. By Treadway, you think?"

"Who else?"

"Then give me answers, Mr. Olin. If Treadway has the papers, why doesn't he get out as fast as he can and get them to his employer? Why does he hang around and, late in the day, kidnap Johnny Sassoon? Why does he butcher that girl in Johnny's room? Why does he try to bomb his way to Gamayel? He had succeeded after one murder. Why all the rest? If the papers were his objective, then all I can assume is that he failed in the first place. He didn't get them."

Olin snubbed out his cigarette. The green glasses hid what he was thinking.

"He didn't take off because he didn't have what he was paid to get," Chambrun said. "Now maybe he killed Sassoon, but if he did, the papers were already gone. He isn't sure who's got them, but he tries all the possibilities—perhaps including Mrs. Brent, whom we don't seem to be able to locate at the moment. But any way you figure it, Mr. Olin, that third party you mentioned is involved. He has the papers and he's on his way with them, unconcerned by Treadway's bloody attempts to find them. Who is he?"

Olin seemed to be frozen.

"Could you be on Treadway's target list, too, Olin?"

"I can take care of myself," Olin said, as though he was far away somewhere.

"Treadway has to know we're looking for him and that the police are looking for him. What does he do now? You are a professional. What would you do in his shoes?"

"I wouldn't have got into this mess in the first place," Olin said. "He can't just walk out of the hotel?"

"Not if he was the bomber. No chance after that. And let me point out to you that whoever your third party is, Mr. Olin, he persuaded Gamayel to leave Mark's apartment quite a few minutes before the bombing took place. Why would the third party want Gamayel if Gamayel doesn't have the papers?"

"To keep him from talking to anyone ever again," Olin said.

"Again, who can it be, Mr. Olin? Who should we be looking for? I really can't buy Gamayel himself or Mrs. Brent, you know."

"I need to give it some thought," Olin said.

"There isn't time for thought!" Chambrun said.

TWO

THE ONE THING in the world that Chambrun doesn't want in his hotel was beginning to happen when we hit the lobby. Panic. Hundreds of rooms had already been checked out and guests were swarming around the main desk, ten deep, demanding reassurance, demanding the right to leave the building, demanding the right to check out at once. People were storming the main doors on Fifth Avenue and the two side entrances, only to find their way blocked not only by hotel employees but by the police. Hundreds of normally elegant people were on the verge of becoming involved in an old-fashioned Tenth Avenue brawl.

The minute Chambrun appeared, I thought he was going to be torn to pieces. Men and women grabbed at his clothes, all shouting at him, some hysterical, some angry, all loud!

There's a loud-speaker system in the lobby, used for paging people under normal circumstances. Jerry Dodd and I, along with Mike Maggio, formed a kind of flying wedge to get Chambrun to the desk. Karl Nevers helped him up, so that he was literally standing on the desk, high above the crowd, holding a microphone in his hand. Somehow he managed to get a degree of quiet simply by standing there and waiting. I was searching the faces of the crowd for some sign of

Valerie, but she wasn't there. I saw Emory Clarke somewhere on the fringes.

"Most of you know that I am Pierre Chambrun, the Beaumont's manager," Chambrun said into the speaker system. He spoke so softly they had to quiet down to hear him. He regretted the confusion. He assured them he felt the danger was over, but that the criminal responsible for the second-floor bombing was still somewhere in the hotel. It might take another forty-five minutes to cover the building from top to bottom. People who were known to us were free to leave, but the hotel and the police would have to have a list of everyone who chose to go out. This would be a slow and irritating process. "Meanwhile," he told them, "the bars and late night restaurants will be kept open and whatever you need to revive your spirits will be on the house. Believe me, the inconvenience is only part of our effort to protect you from any conceivable danger. If all of you try to check out, it will take hours. So eat, drink, and be merry—and try to forgive us for the trouble."

Somebody started to applaud and the tension seemed to break a little. We helped Chambrun down from his precarious perch on the desk. People began to move, almost happily, toward the bars and the Blue Lagoon. By the time he handed out several hundred free drinks, free food, and paid the staff overtime, this night was going to cost Chambrun plenty.

Chambrun and I went out through the office behind the desk to avoid the crowd and up the fire stairs to the second floor. Miss Ruysdale was at her desk, buried under floor plans for the entire building.

"Better than half the floors have reported in," she told Chambrun. She smiled. "Only five lawsuits threatened so far. Nothing found, and no one has seen anyone matching Treadway's description or Gamayel's."

"Put Mrs. Valerie Brent on that wanted list," Chambrun said.

"You have a very agitated Mr. Carlson in your office," Miss Ruysdale said.

"I thought you fed him sleeping pills," Chambrun said.

"Evidently they don't work on him."

Carlson was far from the dapper lawyer we'd first met early yesterday. He needed a shave, and his eyes looked sunk in their sockets.

"I've got to get out of here, Mr. Chambrun," he said.

"You've heard something?" Chambrun asked.

"No!" He seemed to have trouble controlling his face. The corners of his mouth twitched. "You don't really expect to hear anything now, do you? It's hours since they cut out on us. God help Johnny!"

"You're the man they'll want to talk to," Chambrun said. He glanced at the black suitcase behind his desk. "You're the money man. Have you thrown in the towel on Johnny?"

"Anybody can take instructions from them if they ever do call," Carlson said. "Do you have any idea what kind of a madhouse is going on in our offices?"

Chambrun glanced at his wrist watch. "At one o'clock in the morning?"

"That's the time here," Carlson said. "The time is different in London and Berlin and Moscow and Hong Kong. I know we're being swamped with inquiries, demands for decisions. Our whole business world can collapse on us if we don't have the right answers. I simply have to get to the office."

"And Johnny goes down the drain?"

Carlson twisted his head from side to side. "If Johnny is alive, if he comes out of it, his future may depend on what happens at the office in the next few hours. When the stock market opens in the morning, there'll be a panic if we haven't made plans to avert it."

Chambrun hesitated for a moment, his eyes narrowed as if he was trying to read Carlson's mind. "What do you want us to do with the money?" he said.

"Keep it here," Carlson said. "They may want someone to deliver it quickly."

Chambrun nodded. "All right," he said. "Mark, take Mr. Carlson downstairs and arrange for the people on the doors to let him out."

"Some other time I'll thank you for what you've tried to do," Carlson said.

"The doing still lies ahead of us, Mr. Carlson," Chambrun said.

THE LOBBY LOOKED LESS like the *Titanic* going down than it had a few minutes ago. There are always some people who insist on having their way no matter how easy you make it for them not to. Karl Nevers at the desk was trying to appease them. I managed to get

Carlson to a side exit presided over by one of Jerry's men. They took down the lawyer's name, address, and phone number and bowed him out.

Back in the lobby I bumped into Emory Clarke, his Charles Laughton face crinkled with amusement. "Free drinks will work miracles on people's courage," he said. "Any real progress?"

I told him that except for Olin we hadn't come up with any of the people we were looking for.

"Nothing more from the kidnappers?" he asked. "Perhaps I shouldn't ask, but seeing you usher Ray Carlson out of the building, I wondered."

"Nothing since eight o'clock," I said. "Carlson's having a nervous breakdown over tomorrow morning's stock market."

"He could be right," Clarke said. He inhaled on his cigarette. "I'm pretty well pooped out," he said. "I don't know what it might be, but if there's any way I can help, I'll be in my room. I take it you found Val?"

"Not yet."

He frowned. "Not in her room?"

"Not when it was searched."

"Oh, well, you'll find she went out to join some friends somewhere."

"Not if you took her to her room when you left my place," I said. "By then every exit was blocked off—Chambrun's orders."

"There could have been a slip-up in the first few minutes," he said.

"Don't let Chambrun hear about it," I said.

"I wouldn't sweat over it," he said. "In all the excitement somebody could have turned his back for a moment. She didn't know she wasn't supposed to go out.''

I watched his shaggy gray head move through the crowd that still milled around the lobby toward the elevators. I made my way to one of the house phones and called Valerie's room. Still no answer. Well, in a little while there wasn't going to be a broom closet that hadn't been searched. She had to show up unless Clarke was right.

As I turned away from the phone, I saw Karl Nevers trying to flag me. I edged my way over to the desk.

"The switchboard's flooded with calls from the media," he said. "Newspapers, TV and radio. The boss gave orders no one was to be let in except registered guests. We can't shut them out forever. Too many people have been given the green light to leave. Everything but the truth has been leaked to the outside by now. What do we tell them?''

I had no instructions from Chambrun about the media. I went back up to the second floor to get orders. Miss Ruysdale was still surrounded by her floor plans.

"Only two floors and the basements unreported," she told me. "No luck so far."

I went into Chambrun's office and found Lieutenant Hardy with him. In the midst of all the confusion the Homicide man had been going doggedly about his business—catching a murderer. He'd now checked out the fingerprint evidence with one exception—the thumbprint on the headboard of J. W. Sassoon's bed. The other sets of prints in the old man's room belonged to Johnny and the room service waiter. Item

two, the gun Olin had been carrying was not, as I suspected, the one that had killed Trudy. Item three, one
of Hardy's men had noticed Treadway leave the Trapeze shortly after Gamayel and I had gone up to
Chambrun's office. Treadway had headed for the elevators. The man had no particular reason to pay attention to Treadway until he got a description of him
later. Item four, the bullet the Medical Examiner had
pried out of poor little Trudy's skull did not match the
ballistics record of the bullet that had killed Michael
Brent two years ago. Same "trademark," as Clarke
had called it, but not the same gun.

"Item five," Hardy said, "with Olin alibied, we're
just exactly nowhere until we can lay hands on Treadway or Gamayel. I'd just about decided that Treadway and Olin were fighting a war in our line of
country, but with that Washington alibi—"

"Don't write off the idea," Chambrun said. "A war
is what's going on, and Treadway and Olin will do till
we come up with some more likely antagonists." He
waved smoke from his cigarette away from his face.
"I've said it many times, but it's worth saying again.
In this day and age, with life so cheap, the man who
pulls the trigger is only a minor character in the
drama. The killer-shark is out of sight, in deep water.
Treadway and Olin are sophisticated technicians, but
in the final analysis they are paid mercenaries. You
may put one or both of them in jail, Hardy, but I'm
after the killer-sharks myself."

"Who would appear to be thousands of miles away
in the Middle East," Hardy said.

"Maybe," Chambrun said. "Just maybe."

I pulled myself together and told Chambrun why I was there. The press. The media. How did we handle them?

"Normally I'd say tell them nothing that would disturb the peace in the hotel," Chambrun said. "It's too late for that. I'd say give them the works for once—if Hardy agrees."

Hardy shrugged. "Draw up a statement, Mark, and I'll sign it. Hand it out to them, but no interviews yet. Two murders, a kidnapping and a bombing ought to keep them busy for a while," His smile was sour. "It may also find me pounding a beat on Staten Island when the Commissioner reads it!"

I remember I reached in my pocket for a cigarette and found something unfamiliar along with the pack. It was a slip of paper I hadn't seen before. I frowned at it, trying to figure it out.

"What is it, Mark?" Chambrun asked. He'd read the look on my face.

"A telephone number," I said.

"Whose number?"

"You've got me," I said. "It's not something I wrote down—not my writing."

"Where did you get it?"

"Again, I don't know. Somebody must have slipped it in my pocket when I was milling around in the lobby. But why? No instructions. Just the number."

"Call it," Chambrun said, gesturing to one of the phones on his desk.

I picked up one of the phones and asked the switchboard for the number. It rang about four times before someone picked up the receiver on the other end. I felt the small hairs rising on the back of my neck. No one spoke—but it was the breather again. Long, shallow, quavering breaths.

I pointed urgently to the black suitcase beside Chambrun's chair. He hurried toward Miss Ruysdale's office.

"This is Mark Haskell," I said. "I had a message to call."

There was a kind of sigh, and then something that sounded like a sepulchral whisper. "Alone. Phone booth. Fifty-ninth Street. Twenty minutes."

The phone clicked off. The dial tone sounded. There'd been no time for Chambrun to trace it. He came back from the outer office.

"We'll have the telephone company check out the number for us," he said, "but ten to one it's a phone booth somewhere."

"What do I do?"

"Go," he said.

"But you'll be covered," Hardy said, reaching for the phone.

I have to tell you that I was happy to know that somewhere in the shadows behind me as I walked down Fifth Avenue there was someone I could count on. The Avenue was almost deserted. An occasional taxi whizzed past, but I saw only one other pedestrian in the five-block stretch—a woman walking a miniature black poodle.

I got to the phone booth with about three minutes to spare. I couldn't see Hardy's man anywhere, but I took him for granted. Right on the dot the phone rang and I picked up the receiver.

"Mark Haskell here," I said.

"Congratulations on promptness," a brisk voice said. No breathing this time. The voice was, as I say, brisk, energetic, but it sounded as though the man was talking with his mouth full. As though he was eating! Suddenly I thought of that denturelike device Jerry had found in the trash barrel. Olin had called it a voice alterer.

"I take it you have instructions about the money," I said.

"I have instructions, Mr. Haskell," the voice said. "You are to go back to the Beaumont."

"To get the money?"

"Be good enough to let me do the talking, Mr. Haskell." In spite of the mouthful sound it was a cold, hard voice. "You will go back to the hotel. You will inform Mr. Chambrun and the police that you are to go to Mr. Chambrun's penthouse on the roof. But you are not to be watched, or followed, or checked on. You are to go there and wait for instructions."

"By phone?" I asked.

"Just listen, Mr. Haskell. You will take an elevator, alone, to the penthouse level. You will step out of the elevator and you will watch the indicator till you know the elevator has gone down again. You will let yourself into the penthouse with a key which I trust Mr. Chambrun will give you. You will wait, inside the penthouse, for instructions."

"By phone?" I asked again.

"Just listen to me, Mr. Haskell. You were to have come to that phone booth alone. If you'll look across the way to the entrance of a dress shop, you'll see a shadow. That's the man you had follow you. It will be just as easy to check on whether you go to the penthouse alone, without any traps set. If you don't do exactly as you're told, Mr. Haskell, we will provide Mr. Chambrun with a nice dead body to ponder.''

"You're telling me that you'll kill me if I don't obey you?''

The man laughed. "Oh, no. We need you, Mr. Haskell. But you would like to see Mrs. Brent alive again, wouldn't you?''

I CAME OUT OF THAT phone booth for the second time in five hours, wringing wet. I took off on the run toward the shadow in the entrance to the dress shop.

"They spotted you,'' I said to the man.

"Damn! No instructions, then?''

"Oh, I got instructions. Listen, go to that booth and phone Chambrun.'' I gave him the special number. "Tell him not to go to his penthouse, or let anyone else go, until I get back to him and explain.''

I didn't take time to tell him anything more. I started to run back up Fifth Avenue to the Beaumont. In spite of the mouthful-sound of that voice, the threat it conveyed had seemed completely real to me. I tried to concentrate on whether it was a voice I knew, garbled by what I assumed was a voice alterer. It had been crisp and sharp, with an overtone of sardonic humor. It was not like anyone I knew. I thought it might fit the handsome, athletic-looking man in the white dinner jacket I'd seen earlier in the Trapeze. Treadway. The threat was in character with a man we suspected had killed so easily and so violently.

My aim was to get to Chambrun as quickly as possible. I'm in pretty good shape for my thirty-five years, but I had the anxious feeling I might fall flat on my face before I made it. My legs felt rubbery. When I finally persuaded the guards on the Fifth Avenue entrance to the hotel to let me in, the world was spinning around in front of me. I remember that when I got inside I bent over double trying to get some air into my lungs. I had the feeling I couldn't make the one flight of stairs to the second floor, and I stumbled toward the elevators. Faces looked at me out of a kind of haze, I suppose assuming that I was drunk. Somebody took me by the arm and I tried to shake myself loose.

"What the hell's the matter with you?" Mike Maggio asked.

I grabbed hold of him as though he was a life preserver. "I've got to get to the boss," I managed to tell him.

He didn't ask questions, but got me to an elevator and up to the second floor. Miss Ruysdale was standing out in the hall, a worried look on her handsome face.

"We got your message," she said.

I just sort of waved at her and, still hanging onto Mike, I staggered into Chambrun's office. He was standing up beside his desk. Hardy was still there, talking to someone on one of the phones. I remember I sank down into one of the big green leather armchairs and bent forward again, still trying to get air. I was aware that Miss Ruysdale went over to the sideboard and poured me a drink.

"You can die later," Chambrun said in a cold voice. "Would you mind explaining your message?"

I managed to choke it out in bits and pieces, and then I swallowed the drink Ruysdale brought me. I thought I might not have to die after all.

Chambrun and Hardy were staring at each other.

"Carlson!" Chambrun said. "I knew there was something fishy about him, but he talked me out of it."

"I don't follow," Hardy said.

"If people took over the penthouse, they found him there," Chambrun said. "The hell with the stock market. They got rid of him by frightening him into silence."

"Why didn't they keep him as a hostage?" Hardy asked.

"They've got Valerie," I managed to say.

"And used her with Carlson," Chambrun said. "A good guess is that Carlson is to arrange something for them on the outside—getaway plan. A car, a plane, a boat. Because obviously what they're going to demand of us is a way out of the hotel, unmolested by us or by your people, Hardy."

"And the money, if they know about it," Hardy said, looking at the black bag.

"Oh, they know about it," Chambrun said. "They persuaded Carlson to tell them all they needed to know."

"How could they hole-up in your place when it was being searched by your bomb plan?" Hardy asked.

"Because I am an idiot!" Chambrun said. "I didn't expect to find a bomb, you know that. We were looking for people—Treadway, Olin, Gamayel, Mrs. Brent. Carlson was going to be important to us if we heard from the kidnappers. He was close to breaking. I wanted him rested and ready. So I told the roof crew to bypass my place."

"If they aren't the kidnappers up there," Hardy said, "how did they know about the Fifty-ninth Street phone booth?"

"Carlson," Chambrun said. "Carlson babbling his life away."

Hardy reached for a phone. "We'd better get Carlson back here on the double. He can at least tell us exactly how it is up there."

"Mark is going to tell us that," Chambrun said. He looked at me, almost gently. "If it isn't too much to ask of you, Mark."

"Of course I'll go," I said.

"Why must Mark go up there?" Hardy asked. "Why don't they simply tell us what they want on the phone?"

"They've got Mrs. Brent," Chambrun said. "For all we know they've got Gamayel, possibly even Johnny Sassoon. They want someone to see just how strong their position is. They probably want to ask some questions."

"Like what?" I asked.

"What some of the alternative ways out of the hotel are," Chambrun said. "We just play it move by move."

"But you'll let them go, to save Valerie and any other hostages they may have?" I asked.

Chambrun's eyes narrowed. "It's just possible we may be able to bargain," he said. "While you make your journey up there, Mark, I think we should have Olin and Emory Clarke here, Lieutenant. They may be able to tell us just what we have to bargain with."

Under normal conditions the elevators in the hotel become self-service after one o'clock. The elevator operators go off duty. Those operators were still on tonight, but it was agreed I should go up alone. Mike Maggio urged Chambrun to let him ride up with me.

"If they're going to pull any kind of double cross on Mark—" he said.

"I don't think they will," Chambrun said. "They haven't asked him to bring the money on this trip. They must know it's here. For all we know there is someone watching every move we make—someone in the lobby, for example. So I suggest you go downstairs, Mark. Take your time. Mike, you get the operator off a car. Do it noticeably. Then keep your eyes on the house phones. I'll have the switchboard report if there are any calls to the penthouse. Someone may call up to let them know Mark is following instructions. Maybe we can spot whoever it is."

"Right," Mike said.

Chambrun gave me that gentle look again. "Play it cool, Mark," he said. "Listen to their demands. Don't protest. Don't play the hero over Mrs. Brent, if she's there. Take as much time as they will let you. The longer you're there, the more time we have to set up plans and counterplans."

"Counterplans?"

"If the mastermind up there is Treadway, how much do you think you can count on his word? Once he's out with his hostages, how safe will they be, do you think?"

On that cheerful note Mike Maggio and I went down to the lobby. It was still a pretty busy place, but the atmosphere of panic was gone. I could hear the jazz group playing in the Blue Lagoon, and the sounds of laughter. People have a way of getting over crises in a hurry. Mike went over to one of the elevators and talked to the operator, who left the car. I watched, my hand gripping the key Chambrun had given me as I was leaving the office. I had the insane feeling that I might lose it. Tension? God, was I tense!

I glanced at the house phones. Several of them were in use, but I didn't recognize any of the callers. I walked to the elevator, feeling as though I had diver's boots on my feet. I pressed the button for the roof. The doors closed out the lobby and its people, and a faint whirring noise told me we were going up. The floor numbers over the door blinked on and off, on and off. We went up, floor after floor. I had the impulse to stop the car, get out wherever it stopped, and to hell with it. But I could hear that voice on the phone asking me if I wouldn't like to see Valerie alive again.

The car stopped, the doors slid open, and I looked out into the penthouse foyer. It took an effort to move out of the car before the doors closed. I had to hold them open to make it. I turned and looked up at the indicator. The car was going down, automatically—30, 29, 28, 27.

I opened my hand and looked down at my sweaty palm holding the key. I took it in my right hand and approached the door. I put the key in the Yale lock and turned it. The door opened easily and I went in. The first thing I was aware of was that faint, special perfume of Valerie's.

I went through the inner foyer to the living room.

She was sitting on the couch, facing me. Her hands were locked in front of her in her lap. Her lovely face was pale, the skin stretched tight over her high cheekbones. The wide, hazel eyes met mine steadily.

"Thanks for coming, Mark," she said.

"Are you all right?" My mouth was dry, my voice husky.

"Yes."

"Hold it right there, Haskell," the crisp, energetic voice said. There wasn't anything in his mouth now. He stepped out from behind the carved Burmese screen that flanked the couch. It was Treadway, still wearing the white dinner jacket he'd had on in the Trapeze, still smiling as I'd last seen him. Cradled in his arm was a deadly looking machine pistol. "If you have a gun, I suggest you drop it on the table there."

"I don't have a gun," I said.

"Then turn around and face the door," he said. "You won't mind if I make absolutely certain."

I turned and he came up behind me and patted over my clothes, not too gently. I sensed he moved away, although I couldn't hear anything on the thick Persian rug.

"All right, you can turn around. You can even sit down if you like," Treadway said.

I started toward the couch to sit beside Valerie. I wanted to touch her, to make sure she was alive. She looked like a statue.

"Not so close to the lady," Treadway said, still smiling. "I suggest that chair."

I took the chair he indicated. He had moved around behind the couch so that Valerie was between him and me.

"I like your promptness," he said.

"I came as quickly as I could."

"Leaving Mr. Chambrun to gnash his teeth, I suspect."

"He's ready to listen to what you want," I said.

"I should think he might be. I'm sure he knows how little Mrs. Brent's life means to me."

"Who else is here with you?" I asked.

His smile widened. "Isn't Mrs. Brent enough for you?"

I looked at Val. "Who else?" I asked.

She lowered her eyes and shook her head slowly. I couldn't tell whether she was saying there was no one, or that she couldn't talk.

"First of all," Treadway said, "you must have guessed that my main concern is a way out of the hotel, without being blocked, obstructed, or followed, either in the hotel or out of it. With Mrs. Brent, you understand."

"It figures," I said.

"But I don't mean to leave it to you. And by 'you' I don't mean you, Haskell. I mean Chambrun and his police help."

"There are only so many ways out of the hotel," I said.

"I want to know all or any ways that don't involve the lobby or the main entrances," Treadway said. London-based, his card had said. There was a British lilt to his speech. He looked and performed like an actor, like a James Bond kind of romantic hero. And yet all the while I was remembering Trudy Woodson and the story I'd heard about Valerie's husband. If this was the cold-blooded bastard responsible for those atrocities, you didn't take him lightly. Unbelievable, but you damn well better believe.

"I imagine," Treadway went on, "that by this time Chambrun knows something of my history. I know he's talked to Emory Clarke and to Jim Olin. I hope they impressed him."

"He saw Trudy Woodson," I said, and immediately wished I hadn't. The smile froze on his face. His blazing black eyes had murder in them. He raised the machine pistol in a dramatic gesture and squinted along the barrel. It was aimed right at the middle of my forehead.

"Please!" Valerie said in a tight, frightened voice.

Treadway lowered the gun slowly. Then his smile was real again. The sonofabitch was laughing at me. "If I had been you, I wouldn't have waited to see what would happen," he said. "You have only one chance in a situation like that. If you just sit there and do nothing, you're a dead man."

"I meant to imply," I said, trying to keep my voice from shaking, "that Chambrun doesn't underestimate you."

"Good," he said. "Very good. But Chambrun isn't the only factor in this problem. He doesn't have to have certain things spelled out for him. I told you on the phone that if he didn't want to play the game, I would present him with this lady, very dead. Did you make a believer of him?"

"You made a believer of him," I said.

"I repeat. He isn't the only factor. There are other people who would like to prevent my leaving. Jim Olin, for example. And he couldn't care less what happens to Mrs. Brent. There is Gamayel and his friends, whoever they are, and they couldn't care less."

"So you haven't got Gamayel?" I asked.

"I haven't got Gamayel—yet," he said. "Maybe I'm not being clear, Haskell, though I pride myself on my clarity. Chambrun and his policemen might help facilitate my exit, knowing that I wouldn't hesitate to disembowel Mrs. Brent right in front of them. This little gun can blow a hole the size of a grapefruit right in the middle of her handsome navel. They wouldn't like that and I suspect they wouldn't risk it. But Olin is something else again, and so is Gamayel. So in addition to providing me with a way out, Chambrun must also protect me from those two and anyone who may be working for them."

"We don't know where Gamayel is," I said.

"Then let's just say he is everywhere. What I'm getting at is that the way out must be protected every step of the way by Chambrun's security people *and* the police. Clear?"

"Quite clear," I said.

"So when you go back—oh, yes, you are going back unless you try something foolish—when you go back you will work out the one, or two, or three ways Mrs. Brent and I can be escorted out of here in safety. When you come back and present me with those plans, I will decide which one it's to be. And exactly when it's to happen. Understood?"

"Yes."

"Chambrun will also give me assurances that I can believe that there is no way Olin or Gamayel or anyone else can get at me on the way. I will have to believe those assurances."

"I'll tell him."

"And he must understand," Treadway said, "that one false move, one attempt to invade this penthouse from the roof, or from the elevators—I only have to hear something I can't explain—and Mrs. Brent will be shot to pieces, and so will anyone else I see as long as there is life in me to pull this trigger." His smile widened. "I won't ever go peacefully, Haskell. But you see how completely I depend on your American chivalry. Anything to save a beautiful lady."

"How do we know she'll be safe once you get away from the hotel?"

"You don't."

"How can we protect you once you're out on the street—out of the hotel?"

"I didn't tell you, did I? When I decide which way we'll go, I will notify friends and there will be a car waiting. All you have to do is get us across the sidewalk."

"Carlson's getting you a car?" I asked.

"So Chambrun figured that one, did he?" Treadway said. He laughed. "I wish I didn't have to tie Mr. Chambrun's hands. He'd be an exhilarating opponent. Warn him, however, not to interfere with Carlson. The consequences could be distressing for Mrs. Brent."

"Carlson's on your team?" I asked.

"He couldn't help himself, Mark," Valerie said in that faraway voice. "He was told what would happen to me if he refused."

"Is this what you were afraid of when you asked me for help, Val?"

"Oh, my God, no!" she said.

"All right, Mr. Haskell, on your way," Treadway said. "You return when you are ready with the alternative plans. You phone me first—on the private phone. And one more thing."

"Yes?"

"I understand the ransom money for Johnny Sassoon is waiting in Chambrun's office. Seems a pity to have it lie there, fallow. If the kidnappers call again, you can always raise some more cash for them. So bring what you have up here when you come back."

"Wouldn't it be better if Chambrun came with the plans himself?" I asked.

"It's a tempting idea," Treadway said. "He'd make a better hostage than you in some ways. But I think you must be it, Mr. Haskell."

The sweat trickling down my spine felt cold. "You're planning to take me as well as Mrs. Brent?" I said.

"At least as far as the sidewalk, Mr. Haskell. At least that far."

I took a last look at Valerie. The knuckles of her locked hands were white. Her eyes were level, unwavering.

"You don't have to do this for me, Mark," she said.

"Of course I will."

"Because, in the long run—"

"That will be enough, Mrs. Brent. On your way, Mr. Haskell," Treadway said. "As the saying goes, we haven't got all night. And remember, don't try to bargain with me. I won't answer the phone."

I turned away from Valerie because I couldn't bear to look at her. I thought I knew what she was trying to tell me. She didn't expect to survive this no matter what we did.

THREE

IT SEEMED TO TAKE FOREVER for the elevator to come up to the penthouse foyer. I've run up against some pretty tough guys in my time at the Beaumont, but I don't think anyone had ever given me such a chill as Treadway. I could see that smiling bastard pointing his gun at Trudy Woodson, never giving her a chance. Then I could see him ripping off her clothes, dumping her in the bathtub and carving her to pieces. I had the feeling he took joy in violence. How did you stop such a man? I tried not to think ahead. He planned to go out of the hotel with Valerie and me walking ahead of his gun. As far as the sidewalk, he'd said. Would he leave me there to be scraped up in a basket?

The elevator doors opened and I stepped in. Going down, I could feel my stomach churning. Mike Maggio was waiting just outside the doors when I stepped into the lobby.

"You okay?" he asked.

"I'm still in one piece," I said. "It's Treadway. He has Mrs. Brent up there. If there's anyone else, I didn't see them."

This time I had the strength to make it up the stairs to the second floor. Chambrun's office seemed crowded. Hardy was there along with his Sergeant Kramer. There was Jerry Dodd and the head of our engineering crew, a man named Moffet. Olin's green glasses were fixed on me as I came into the room. Miss Ruysdale was standing at Chambrun's elbow where he sat at his desk. But before I could cross the room, I was confronted by Emory Clarke. He grabbed me by the upper arms and I was surprised by the strength in his hands.

"Val?" he said.

"She's there. She's all right for now," I said.

Then it seemed as if everyone started asking questions at once. Chambrun shouted them down. "Let him tell it his way first! Questions later."

"It's Treadway," I told them. "The only other person I saw was Mrs. Brent. He's armed with some kind of machine pistol. Mrs. Brent was sitting on your couch, boss, and he stood behind her the whole time—so that she was always between us. You were right about Carlson. He is supposed to arrange for a getaway car—maybe later a plane."

"He's on Treadway's team?" Clarke asked.

"Not the way I got it," I said. "He was ordered to help or Valerie would get it."

"She hasn't been harmed yet?" Clarke asked.

"Please, Mr. Clarke!" Chambrun said, his voice harsh. "What are his demands, Mark?"

I laid it out for him. Alternate escape routes. Protection against Olin, Gamayel, and whoever. I saw Olin's green glasses glitter in the light from the chandelier as I mentioned his name. I told Chambrun that Treadway would make the choice of the ways out after they were presented. Presumably he would coordinate with Carlson so that the escape car would be waiting. I was to take the ransom money intended for the kidnappers to him. Valerie and I would be hostages to make sure no one tried to double-cross him on the way out.

Everybody started talking at once again after that. Chambrun had beckoned Jerry Dodd and Moffet, the engineer, to him. An interior plan of the hotel was spread out on the desk.

Lieutenant Hardy cornered me, but we were surrounded by Sergeant Kramer, Olin, Emory Clarke, and Miss Ruysdale. Hardy had a folder in his hands and he opened it and took out a picture.

"This Treadway?" he asked.

It was—Treadway wearing riding clothes, standing beside a beautiful lean hunter. The horse was nibbling at Treadway's sleeve as if he was looking for sugar.

"Ox Ridge Hunt Club a couple of years ago," Hardy said. "He won the trophy. The horse was owned by an Egyptian diplomat who was being protected by the Department. He rode that horse over the jumps like he was being chased by the devil. A reckless rider."

"A reckless man," I said. "I want to tell you he has the living hell scared out of me. I halfway accused him of killing Trudy Woodson and I thought he was going to blast me then and there."

"He is certainly the most dangerous operator in the Middle East," Clarke said. "His kind of violence fits the terrorist climate over there. It's believed he engineered the hijacking of an Israeli plane and personally shot several hostages when demands weren't met. It's rumored he masterminded the assassination of Israeli athletes at the nineteen seventy-two Olympics. I must admit I think he is given credit for things he had nothing to do with. But it's expected of him because he's that kind of man."

"He has no police record in this country," Kramer said.

"He's got one now," Hardy said.

Chambrun broke up our huddle and we all crowded around his desk. "Jerry and Moffet and I have come up with three exit routes," he said. "One: he takes the elevator from the penthouse down to the second basement. He bypasses the kitchens that way. The kitchens are staffed and active all night. He walks along the corridor there to the garbage elevators. They lift up right onto the sidewalk outside the hotel. Two: he goes down one flight to the thirtieth floor, walks down the corridor to the freight elevator. He takes that down to the mezzanine. From there he walks down the fire stairs to a fire door that opens out onto the street. Third: he takes that same freight elevator all the way down to the special kitchen off the ballroom. Neither the ballroom nor that kitchen are in use. He crosses the ballroom into the corridor that leads to the south exit on the lobby floor—past a row of shops that are closed."

"All three ways involve clearing short distances of people who just might be there," Jerry said.

"Can be done?" Hardy asked.

"Can be done," Jerry said. "Take us maybe half an hour. We'll have to clear all three areas because we don't know which one he'll choose."

"He needs time, too," Chambrun said. "He has to
let Carlson know where the getaway car is to be waiting, and the car has to get there. These are the only
ways out where we won't have to control a great many
people." He lifted his hooded eyes to James Olin.
"Which one would you choose, Mr. Olin? You're a
professional."

"Number one," Olin said promptly. "He doesn't
have to negotiate the thirtieth floor to get to the freight
elevator. He goes straight down on the elevator that's
right at his door."

"That would be my choice," Chambrun said.
"Except for one thing."

The green glasses focused on him without comment.

"That subbasement is a dark labyrinth," Chambrun said. "We could have twenty men hidden down
there he couldn't see—no matter what we promised
him. We have a better than even chance of getting him
and saving the hostages if he chooses that. The other
ways are brightly lighted, no hiding places for us. He
could see anyone who might threaten him. So, not
being a professional, Mr. Olin, I would choose either
the second or third way. I think the second, because
there might be parked cars, taxis, outside that ballroom exit. As a matter of fact, we could have someone there who could follow the escape car. So my
amateur choice would be number two. Let us hope he
chooses number one."

The thin mouth under the green glasses smiled.
"Your amateur standing is in jeopardy, Chambrun. I
think you're in the big leagues."

Chambrun seemed to have lost interest in him. "Now we have other decisions to make," he said. "First of all, do we go through with any part of it at all?"

"Valerie!" Clarke said, his voice husky.

"Mrs. Brent's chances of surviving this, no matter how we play it, are practically zero," Chambrun said.

"If he gets away safely, he has no need to harm her," Clarke said.

"She probably knows too much about him. Using the private line upstairs, he must have been in communication with his people. She will have overheard. And killing for him is a pleasure, like smoking or drinking for the rest of us. I think Mrs. Brent's chances are almost nil."

"But we have to give her a chance, don't we?" Jerry Dodd asked.

Chambrun looked back at Olin. "What about it, Olin? What are the chances he'll let Mrs. Brent go once he's safely away from the hotel?"

"Maybe you ought to ask Mr. Clarke," Olin said. "He's a close friend and confidante. Mrs. Brent was working against J. W. Sassoon from the inside, pretending she no longer suspected him of being responsible for her husband's murder. How much did she get to know about J.W.'s operation? How much did he brag to her? He was a vain old bastard, vain about his power. My guess is that it was enough to make her more than an attractive woman hostage to Treadway. I think he may be killing two birds with one stone. He uses her to get away, and then he silences a dangerous person to his employers."

"Mr. Clarke?" Chambrun said.

Clarke shook his shaggy head. "Val never told me anything that would confirm that idea," he said. "She wasn't interested in J.W.'s power plays. She was only interested in tracking down her husband's killer."

"And isn't she sitting with that killer in my apartment this very moment? Didn't she see him react to Mark's question? Let her go and Treadway knows she will keep trying to get him. Simpler to eliminate her now, while he's got her."

"You still have to give her a chance," Clarke said.

"Let's be realists and not sentimentalists," Chambrun said. "We have a brutal killer in our power. He can't get away without our help. We help him because he threatens to kill Mrs. Brent. But we know that after we've helped him, he will kill her anyway."

"We have to risk that," Clarke insisted.

Chambrun's eyes turned to me. "Does Mark have to risk his life against those odds? 'As far as the sidewalk' Treadway said. What then? 'Thanks, old boy,' and take off? No, gentlemen, I say if we are realists we get an army of cops up on the roof, bulletproof vests, helmets—tear gas. We smoke him out, and if he turns his little machine pistol on us, we let him have it."

"Valerie's chances?" I asked.

"Just as good that way as they are the other. Zero," Chambrun said, his voice flat and hard. "So do we help a killer escape, or do we take him?"

"Mr. Chambrun?" It was Betsy Ruysdale. "If I were up there instead of Mrs. Brent, would you— would you write me off so easily?"

"I would probably be sentimental about you, God help me," Chambrun said, not looking at her.

"So we have to give Valerie a chance," Clarke said. "You're playing tough, Chambrun, but I know that at heart you're a decent person."

"So I hear," Chambrun said. "So we let Mark risk his life for the nonexistent chance Mrs. Brent has?"

I could feel my heart pounding against my ribs. It was not that I hoped they'd tell me I couldn't go. I was beginning to realize what it meant. My chance was about zero, too. What am I saying? Of course I hoped I wouldn't have to go! But I would go if I had to.

Chambrun looked at me, and in those buried eyes of his I saw that this tough, irascible man cared what happened to me. "Ruysdale chose to put this on a personal level," he said. "She and I have been—been very close for a long time." It was the nearest I'd ever heard him come to admitting that there was more than an employer-secretary relationship there. "I guess I would give her the chance to live a little while longer, since living is the only thing we really cherish. Mrs. Brent is a beautiful, desirable, electric woman. You wouldn't be a man if she hadn't stirred you physically. But in the long run she doesn't mean a damn thing to you, Mark. Would you risk your life for any woman who was in trouble? If you would, you're an idiot!"

"I think there may be an out from this dilemma, Mr. Chambrun," Clarke said. We all turned to look at him. His face was twisted into an expression of almost wry humor. "I have known Valerie for a long time. I care for her. If I were younger, I would long ago have tried to persuade her to share her life with me. Let me go in Mark's place. Let me be the second hostage. Oh, I want to go on living just as much as Mark does, but he has the best of a lifetime ahead of him. I have a relatively short time. And—and I care for Valerie.''

"My God, how noble everybody is," Chambrun said, not as moved as I was. "Wouldn't I be the best hostage, when it comes to that? The whole staff would be sure not to interfere with him then. I've wondered why he didn't suggest it."

"Because you are the only person he can be sure will protect him—if you say you will," Olin said.

"Call him and ask him if he will accept me in Mark's place," Clarke said.

"He won't answer the phone. He told me that," I said.

"If someone unexpected walks in on him, he may not wait to ask why," Olin said.

"Your advice in invaluable, Mr. Olin," Chambrun said, anger in his voice again. "I don't ask you to go, Mark. I advise against it on the grounds that it is sheer madness. But since the consensus seems to be that Mrs. Brent should be given a chance, the decision is yours."

"I'll go," I said.

Chambrun looked away, and he never looked at me again until a long time later. "There is a third element to this that we haven't discussed," he said. "How can we protect him from people we don't control? He mentioned Olin, Gamayel, and a possible third party. We can keep Mr. Olin out of circulation,

but we don't know who may be working for him. We
don't know where Gamayel is. A thorough search of
the hotel hasn't turned him up. We don't know who
may be working for *him*. We have no leads at all to
who a third party may be. Any suggestions, Olin?''

"J.W. had so many enemies," Olin said. He
shrugged.

Chambrun drew a deep breath. "Then we prepare
the three avenues of escape. That's for you, Jerry.
He'll need help from your people, Hardy."

The Lieutenant nodded. "The whole world today
seems to operate on blackmail through hostages," he
said. "It's probably happening in a dozen other places
around the globe at exactly this moment. We're getting used to it in the Department. I stand by and let a
killer slip through my fingers like water."

"I don't have too much hope that Treadway will
take our subbasement route," Chambrun said.
"That's the place where we station a few men who can
do better than hit a barn door with a gun. We just
might take him there. The other two routes we simply
clear away people and let him go. That means the
thirtieth floor, the fire stairs on the mezzanine, the
ballroom kitchen, and the ballroom, and the passage
past the shops to the side exit. I think you'd better get
moving, gentlemen."

Jerry, Hardy, and Sergeant Kramer started out. At
the door Jerry turned back. We were old friends.
"Good luck, man," he said.

"Thanks," I said. I noticed that my hands felt cold.

Chambrun turned to Miss Ruysdale. "Mark had
better take these floor plans with him," he said. He

was deliberately not talking to me. "He should tell
Treadway that it will take us at least a half hour to set
things up. And he should not forget to take the
money."

He got up from his desk and walked out of the office after Jerry and the others. Not a word or a look.

"You matter to him, Mark," Miss Ruysdale said.

I have to confess my head was swimming a little. It's
one thing to talk about a problem: what you should
do, who you should give a chance to, how you handle
a wild animal. But when you suddenly decide to be a
hero and walk into a cage with that animal, it's something else again. I remember when they sent me to
fight in the war in Vietnam I was pretty damned bitter. The people in the government, from the President
on down, were being pretty damned free with my life,
my body. I didn't believe in the war, but I had no
choice, and the bastards who were sending me didn't
have to sit up to their armpits in a jungle swamp waiting for a sniper to blow off their heads.

Now I was walking into something I didn't have to
walk into. All I had to do was turn to Chambrun and
Hardy and tell them to work it out. It wasn't my
problem; it wasn't my obligation. And then I thought
how outraged I'd been when I'd read in the paper
about dozens of people standing around watching a
woman being beaten to death by a mugger, not one of
them lifting a finger to help or even bothering to call
the police. They didn't want to get involved. I remember thinking at that time that being involved was
all there was to living.

There was a chance for Valerie, I told myself. It wasn't going to come in the subbasement where Hardy would have his hidden snipers. It wasn't going to come on the thirtieth floor, or in the freight elevator, or on the fire stairs or the ballroom exit. Treadway would be a hundred percent ready in all those places. The chance could come in the half hour we waited to take off from the penthouse. I was an errand boy, I wasn't armed, I was laughably concerned for Valerie. *I wasn't dangerous!* There could be ten seconds of carelessness, ten seconds when Treadway would turn his back on me. In that ten seconds I would have to be dangerous as all hell. No hesitation because I was a decent guy. That, I told myself, was going to be my only chance and Valerie's—ten seconds of carelessness by Treadway before we actually moved out into the danger areas as he saw them.

I became aware of Ruysdale standing next to me. She had the floor plans rolled up with a rubber band around them.

"You may not believe it, but I know him better than you do, Mark." I knew she was talking about Chambrun. "He isn't going to let you down without a struggle."

"What can he do? All he has to do is blink his eyes and Treadway will mow us down. He doesn't make idle threats."

"I've seen Pierre up against insoluble problems many times," she said. "I've come to believe that he always comes up with an answer."

I gave her a sickly grin. "There has to be a first time for everything," I said.

She handed me the rolled-up floor plans and reminded me there was also the suitcase to take. Olin and Clarke joined us where we stood.

"I'm sorry, Mark," Clarke said. "I would have been glad to go. I think I wanted to go—to be with Valerie."

Olin's green glasses glittered at me. "You are a prize sucker, friend," he said. "You're dreaming there may be some way to get him before the exodus starts, aren't you?"

"You have to dream, I guess," I said.

"I always look for an edge when it comes to a showdown," he said. "Some very small thing sometimes gives you a crucial edge. I've been trying to think of something that would help you. I have a book on Treadway—in my head. Your only chance is just about hopeless."

"What's my only chance?"

"What you've been thinking," Olin said. "To catch him off guard, close with him, and fight it out. Are you any good?"

"I was a Marine commando—a long time ago," I said.

"Treadway eats Marine commandos for breakfast," Olin said. "He knows all the tricks, all the dirty tricks. He's a karate expert. He fights to kill, friend, not just to protect himself. I can only think of one edge for you. It's not enough, but it's all I know to tell you. He searched you when you went in, didn't he?"

"Yes."

"So you can't carry a knife or a gun. He'll search you again."

"And the edge you mentioned?"

"It's really nothing. It's hardly worth mentioning," Olin said. "For what it's worth, he's left-handed. If he swings at you, it will be with his left. He will reach for a gun with his left hand. If you know karate moves, his will be the opposite of normal. It isn't much of an edge, friend, but it's all I've got."

Ruysdale was holding out the suitcase to me. It was time to go. "Watch for the smallest thing," she said. "Pierre will try something."

"Good luck," Clarke said.

God knows I wanted to stall, but there was no point. I had a date with a killer and I had to keep it.

FOUR

CARRYING THE SUITCASE and the rolled-up floor plans, I walked down to the lobby once more. Things had really quieted down. I flagged Mike Maggio and once more he got the operator off the roof car for me, and I started my trip up, alone and about as scared as I've ever been in my life. I learned something in the Marines about being scared. I thought I was the only one at first and I was ashamed of it. After a while I found out that the few who weren't scared were the dumdums of the outfit. Any man with any imagination at all is scared when the danger is real. The ones who don't run away are the brave guys. The dumdums aren't brave, they're just stupid.

Drowning men, they say, see their whole lives go by them as they're going down for the last time. I was seeing a lot of mine—going up!

I arrived at the penthouse level much sooner than I wanted to. I got out of the elevator and stood looking at the indicator, watching the car go down. I never felt so goddamned alone in my whole life.

I turned and faced the door to the penthouse. I thought of ringing the bell, and then I decided Treadway would expect me to use the key again. I fumbled for it in my pocket, inserted it in the lock, and let myself in.

"Treadway! It's me," I called out.

"Who else? Come in, Haskell."

Valerie was still sitting on the couch and I saw that there was a drink on the coffee table in front of her. Treadway was standing at the stretcher table that backed up on the couch. His machine pistol was resting on the table, right by his left hand, I saw.

"Put down your luggage, Haskell," he said. "I don't suppose you'd have been foolish enough to arm yourself, but turn around so I can make sure."

I put down the suitcase and turned around. He came up behind me, soundless on the thick rug, and went over me once more with his rough hands.

"All right, you can turn around," he said. He'd taken the suitcase, I saw, and had it in front of him on the table. He opened it and threw up the lid. "What a magnificent sight. Have you ever seen half a million dollars in cold cash, Haskell?"

I hadn't. I didn't much care. I was looking at Valerie, hoping she might see something reassuring in me. I thought the tension had brought her very near some kind of breaking point.

"Chambrun and the police have agreed," I told her. "There won't be any trouble." I hoped it hadn't occurred to her that Treadway meant to kill her anyway, once they were out of the hotel.

"You shouldn't have come back for me, Mark," she said, her voice husky. "You shouldn't have put yourself in danger."

"Let's get down to business," Treadway said, closing the suitcase. "I take it that roll you're carrying is a floor plan."

"Yes. Chambrun has suggested three ways out. You can follow them on the plan if you want."

"Toss it over," he said.

It clearly wasn't his intention to let me get very close to him. I tossed the roll of floor plans over the end of the couch. He caught them, with his left hand, I noticed. He spread them out on the table.

"Tell me," he said.

I started to walk toward him with the idea of pointing the routes out to him on the plans—and getting close to him.

"Tell me from where you are," he said, smiling at me.

The sonofabitch knew. He knew what I had in mind and he was laughing at me.

I described the first way: the elevator outside the door here to the subbasement. A walk along the corridor to the garbage lifts. Up onto the sidewalk. You've seen those garbage elevators outside big city buildings. There are iron doors at the sidewalk level and the elevator lifts them up as it surfaces. I told him about the two other ways, both of which required walking along a corridor on the thirtieth floor to the freight elevator.

"The freight elevator doesn't come up to the roof?" he asked.

"No. But the corridor on thirty will have been cleared."

I went on to describe the mezzanine fire stair out, and the ballroom side exit out. "These are the only ways that won't involve a lot of people." I hesitated. "The number one way seems the best to all of us. You

take the elevator right outside the door here. It takes
you right to the subbasement with no stops—no
chance of anyone accidentally walking into the picture. The one or two employees on the engineering
staff who might be in that subbasement will have been
removed. I lead you to the garbage elevator and you're
up on the street in thirty seconds. You can see on those
plans where the garbage lift comes up on the street.
You can have your car waiting there. A few feet across
the sidewalk and you have it made.''

He looked down at the plan, tracing the course with
his finger. Then he looked up at me and smiled his
brightest smile.

"It looks perfect," he said. "Except for one thing."

"What's that?" I asked.

"You want me to choose it," he said.

I'd done it. I'd been too eager to point out the ad-
vantages.

"It appears to me that there would be all kinds of
places in that subbasement for Chambrun and the
police to hide people. No, Haskell, you'll have to get
up a lot earlier in the morning to get me to walk into
such a transparent trap."

I had the sick feeling that if I hadn't said anything,
he might have fallen for it.

"I think I like the way down to the mezzanine on the
freight elevator and then down the fire stairs to the
street," Treadway said.

I didn't tell him that would have been Chambrun's
choice. The safest way, the surest way.

Treadway laughed. "I read you like a child's primer,
Haskell. That's the way you hoped I wouldn't choose,

therefore the best way. So let's get into motion. First, you call your people on the house phone and tell them the choice I've made. I will call Carlson on the private line and tell him where to send the car." He gestured toward the house phone which was on a small table just to my right. "I think we need half an hour to be sure of the car." He glanced at his watch. "Twenty minutes past two. Tell your people we will walk out of here at exactly ten minutes to three."

He watched me go to the house phone, and the minute I picked it up, he began dialing a number on the private phone which rested right beside him on the stretcher table. I heard him ask for Carlson, and then Miss Ruysdale was on my line and I didn't hear the rest of what he said.

"It's Mark," I said. "The man has made his choice. Freight elevator to the mezzanine and then the fire stairs."

"Chambrun thought he would," she said.

"We walk out of here at exactly ten minute to three."

"You're all right, Mark?"

"So far."

"Mrs. Brent?"

"So far."

"Is he listening?"

"No, he's on the private line."

"Don't try anything, Mark. Leave it to Chambrun."

I heard myself give out with an inane giggle. "You're just a woman in love," I said.

"Which means complete trust," she said quite seriously. "Don't try anything at all until there's absolutely no chance of help."

"Too bad I didn't bring my needlepoint with me," I said. "It would have helped pass the time. Remember, we move in—twenty-eight minutes."

I put down the phone and found Treadway watching me. "Cooperation?" he asked.

"Do they have a choice?" I asked.

"Not if they care for your precious skins," he said. "Care for some whiskey? It may be a long time between drinks." He gestured toward the portable bar.

I wanted a drink quite badly. I looked at Valerie's empty glass. "For you?" I asked.

"Scotch on the rocks," she said.

I took her glass and went over to the little bar. While I fumbled around with ice cubes, bottles, and glasses I thought about Ruysdale's advice. It was obvious that Treadway knew exactly what was on my mind. He wasn't going to let me get close enough to him to make any sudden move. Perhaps in the elevators, or in the narrow confines of the fire stairs—

He never took his eyes off me as I carried Valerie's glass back to the coffee table. He was not a man who would let down his guard for a moment. I took a swallow of the bourbon I'd poured myself.

"Let's talk about what happens when the time comes," Treadway said.

"Which time? The time when we leave or the time when you kill us?" When it looks like you can't win, you get a little reckless.

"Now, now, Mr. Haskell, don't be bitter," he said, smiling. "First let's talk about the time when we leave. We'll go out of here in single file to the elevator. You will go first, Haskell, carrying all that green money. Mrs. Brent will follow you. I will be directly behind her with my gun pressed against the back of her head firmly enough so that she'll be quite aware of it. You will ring for the elevator, Haskell. When the door opens, you will walk into the far left-hand corner, as you face it. Clear?"

"Quite clear," I said, and took another swallow of my drink. Dutch courage, my father used to call it.

"Mrs. Brent will walk right back into the center of the car. I will deploy to her right. Then we will all face the door. We go down one flight to the thirtieth floor. The door opens, you go out first, Haskell. We follow in the same order. You lead us directly to the freight elevator which I trust will be there, ready for us. I loathe waiting."

"It'll be there," I said.

"We go into the freight elevator in the same fashion, you to the left, Mrs. Brent between us in the center. Same procedure on the way out at the mezzanine. You lead us to the fire stairs and out onto the street, where the car will be waiting."

"And then?" I asked.

His smile widened. "If all has gone well, Mrs. Brent and I will get into the car and wave goodbye. You will, of course, open the car door for us. I want you close enough to deal with you in case there is any last-minute betrayal."

"What happens to Mrs. Brent then?" I asked.

"I'm afraid you'll have to wait and see, old man."
He glanced at his watch. "A little less than twenty
minutes. If you two would like a few intimate words
together, I have no objection. I don't drink when I'm
working, so I'm going to make myself a cup of coffee. Bear in mind that, with the door open, I can see
you quite clearly from the kitchenette. I once shot a
man right between the eyes from a window across the
street. The range here is laughably shorter."

He picked up his machine pistol and walked straight
back into the kitchenette. I know I thought of grabbing Valerie and trying to race out of there while he
reached for a jar of instant coffee in the cupboard. At
the same moment I knew how hopeless it was. The
elevator wouldn't be waiting there, and there'd be noplace to go except out onto the roof. We'd be sitting
ducks for him out there. This wasn't the moment for
heroics.

"I can't think of anything to say to you, Val, except clichés—like where there's life there's hope."

"Poor Mark," she said. "Dear Mark."

"How did he get hold of you?"

"He came to my room, knocked on the door. I
thought it was you—I hoped it was you. I opened the
door and he whisked me up here."

"Do you know who he's working for?"

She shook her head. "Long, long ago—like last
night at dinner—Emory pointed him out to me. A very
dangerous man who works for Middle East power
groups. He wondered if he might have had something
to do with J.W.'s death and the theft of Mr. Gamay-

el's documents. Emory said he was a professional killer."

"He is," I said.

She looked at me, her lips parted. "We don't have any chance, do we, Mark? He'll use us and then do away with us?"

"I think that's his plan. It just may not work."

"What's to stop him?" she asked, her eyes widening.

"I believe in miracles," I said. "I have a friend who can sometimes walk on water."

"Mr. Chambrun?"

"He's been known to do the impossible."

She was silent for a moment, looking down at the drink she was holding in her hand. "I don't think you can imagine what it's like to live under the threat of violence every day of your life," she said finally. "It's been that way with me ever since the day Michael was murdered, two years ago. The police bungled it. I was determined to find the killer myself. I knew they wouldn't do anything to me unless I came on the truth. I'd made so much noise about J.W. that if anything happened to me the police would head directly to him. But I knew if I stumbled on the truth they'd have to act. The man Olin, who works for J.W., is just as cold-blooded as this one. Can you understand, Mark, that I have been prepared to die every day of my life for the last two years? Now that it's here, I'm ready to face it. But it shouldn't have involved you."

"Olin was watching you," I said. "He was watching you when you bought those things at Charlene's

Boutique. He says you never went into the park, that no one stole them from you."

"He lies, of course," she said. "J.W. was flattered when I changed my attitude toward him. He was flattered and he felt safe from me. Olin never believed my act. He knew exactly what I was trying to do. He'd like to get me, even now. Well, he isn't going to have to try."

There wasn't time for any more. Treadway came out of the kitchenette balancing a coffee cup in his right hand, holding his gun in his left. I wanted to tell her how beautiful she was, that I was prepared to go the limit for her—and would make a try, once, before it was too late. Somewhere between here and the escape car I would try. What did I have to lose? Treadway gave me the feeling he was looking forward to the moment when he'd wipe me out.

"About six minutes to go," he said cheerfully. "Do we need to go over the game plan again?"

I could feel my stomach muscles tightening. I told myself I was going to have to stay loose if I was to give it any kind of a try. My mouth was dry, and I swallowed the last of my drink. It seemed to burn, unnaturally, going down.

Treadway put down his coffee cup on the stretcher table. He played with his machine pistol, as if to get it comfortable. He stood looking at his watch, like an officer waiting to give the command to attack.

"Here we go," he said at last. "You pick up the bag and face the front door, Mr. Haskell."

He was halfway across the room. If I was ever to have a chance, it was going to come in close quarters.

I should have made it clear to Valerie that when I made a move, she should run for it. I might keep him busy for just long enough. So it couldn't be in the elevators. The corridors, the fire stairs, or even out on the sidewalk. It would have to come in one of those places.

I picked up the suitcase, marveling at how light a half million dollars felt. I faced the door.

"Now, Mrs. Brent," I heard Treadway say. Then: "Mrs. Brent is right behind you, Haskell, and I have my gun pressed against the back of her head. So march."

I didn't look back. I didn't doubt it was just as he said it was. I moved forward to the front door and went out into the foyer.

"Press the elevator button," Treadway said, "and pray to God they've left this car on automatic for us."

I looked up at the indicator. The car was starting up from the lobby. Floor after floor it came up, the indicator making a little clicking noise as it passed each level. I used to be impatient, waiting for that rise. Now it seemed to be happening all too quickly.

The elevator door opened.

"Into the left-hand corner, facing the rear wall, Haskell," Treadway said.

I went in and stood where I was told. I heard the door close.

"Turn around," Treadway said.

Valerie was next to me, close enough to touch. Treadway was next to her, his gun held against her head, just as he'd said. There wasn't a sign that Valerie might crumble. She stood straight and brave.

The car stopped almost at once at thirty.

"Out, Haskell," Treadway said.

I stepped out into the main corridor. I heard the elevator start down. Behind the doors on either side of us were sleeping people—or waiting people. I had to believe that Chambrun was having us watched, even though he couldn't make a move. I could hear the indicator clicking as the car went down.

"You lead the way to the freight elevator, Haskell. Bear in mind that one false move means Mrs. Brent is dead—and you one second later."

There was going to be no miracle here. I walked along the corridor to the far end where the freight elevator was located. It was standing there with its door open. The door on the freight car doesn't work automatically. You have to open and close it manually.

I went into the car and presently I heard the door being closed. I turned around as we started down.

"Your Mr. Chambrun has arranged things very nicely," Treadway said.

Down we went to the mezzanine. The mezzanine is taken up entirely by offices. They were all closed at this time of night. I led the way to the fire stairs. I realized that the only place where I'd have a chance and where Valerie would have a chance was out on the sidewalk. I was to open the door of the getaway car for them. He would have to come close to me to get in. That was probably the moment when I was to get it. That was when I would move.

We went down the fire stairs, our footsteps echoing on the cement steps. The door opening onto the street was operated by a heavy brass bar stretching across it. It opened out to conform to the law.

"You'll open the door, Haskell, and assure me that the car is waiting there," Treadway said.

I felt, suddenly, breathless. The door was heavy. I thought it would have been difficult for a woman or a child to open it. I thought I'd have to point out to Chambrun that something should be done about it. I almost laughed at the idea.

I got the door about half open and saw a black limousine parked directly opposite at the curb. The side street isn't too brightly lit, but I could see the driver sitting at the wheel.

"There's a car," I said.

"Move out then," Treadway said.

The night air felt suddenly fresh. I saw a blurred moon, surrounded by haze, high in the sky. The driver in the car turned his head to look at us. I couldn't see his face.

"You'll move forward and open the rear door of the car," Treadway said. "Toss in the suitcase."

I thought my legs wouldn't work. My moment was seconds away.

I was about a yard from the car when a figure rose up from the far side of the hood. The driver didn't move.

"You'll drop the gun, Treadway, or I'll blast you right through your lady friend," a cold voice said.

I saw who it was. I saw the green glasses. I saw the rifle raised to his shoulder.

"You can't do that, Olin! For Christ sake!" I said.

"He can do it and with my blessing."

I turned my head. Chambrun stood a few yards away, hands jammed in the pocket of his coat.

"Move away, Mark," he said. "Over here toward me. Don't bother with the suitcase."

"You can't let him do it!" I shouted.

Something hit me from my blind side. It was a flying tackle the velocity of which you wouldn't believe. I hit the concrete pavement so hard I thought I was going to black out. I struggled feebly with my tackler.

"Take it easy, man," Jerry Dodd said.

Somehow I wrenched around, horrified by what I thought would happen. Treadway would blow Valerie's head off. Instead I saw him give her a violent shove away from him, saw her go down on her knees. At that moment there was a fusillade of gunshots that sounded like the Battle of the Bulge. Treadway seemed to do a grotesque dance, like a jumping jack on a string. Then he was sitting against the building, a fountain of blood coming out of his mouth. It must all be some kind of a nightmare, I thought, because I saw Lieutenant Hardy pounce on Valerie, yank her to her feet and tear her handbag away from her. She seemed to be screaming obscenities at him. I couldn't believe what I was hearing.

I think I passed out for a moment right about then. Having it come to an end had pulled my cork, I guess.

I OPENED MY EYES and found Chambrun kneeling beside me. In the background there was an ambulance siren.

"You went down pretty hard," Chambrun said.

"What in God's name is going on?" I said.

"Treadway's run out his string," Chambrun said. "Come on, boy. Pull yourself together and come up to the office. It's really quite a story."

He helped me to stand up. Cops and a couple of ambulance people were crowded around Treadway. I didn't see Valerie anywhere. A few feet away Jerry Dodd was rubbing his shoulder.

"I don't know if it was you or the concrete," he said.

I saw Olin talking to the driver of the car.

"You'd have let him shoot her," I said to Chambrun. "What have you done with her?"

"Hardy's taken her away," Chambrun said in a cold voice. "I hope you don't have to see her again, boy."

"I'd have bet my life Treadway would shoot her," I said.

"You'd have lost," Chambrun said. "Don't let it get you down, boy, but Treadway was her lover."

I KNEW THEN I was hallucinating. None of this was happening. I let Chambrun lead me into the side entrance and to the elevators. We went up to his office. The shocks weren't over. Miss Ruysdale met us at the door, touched a bruise on my forehead tenderly, kissed my cheek.

"They're all here," she said to Chambrun, "except Hardy and the woman. Kramer is in charge of the other prisoners."

I followed Chambrun into the office. I still didn't believe it. Emory Clarke was sitting in one of the green leather armchairs. Olin was standing at one of the windows, looking out at the night through his green-tinted lenses. They weren't a surprise. But Mr. Gamayel, smiling his very white smile, was. And Johnny-baby Sassoon, looking white and shrunken, was a shocker. But even that was topped, because I saw that Kramer was standing behind Emory Clarke's chair and that there was a pair of handcuffs on the diplomat's wrists. Clarke!

Chambrun gave me a little pat on the shoulder and moved around behind his desk.

"It's all over, gentlemen," he said. "The police shot down Treadway. Mad dog treatment. Lieutenant Hardy has taken Mrs. Brent into custody. I assume you're not going to make a statement without your lawyer, Mr. Clarke?"

Clarke spoke from the bottom of a deep well somewhere. The voice could have been coming from his own tomb. "Not an official statement," he said. "I would like to say something to Johnny." He turned his shaggy head and I saw that his eyes were red, as if he'd been crying. "Listen to my advice, son," he said. "Take what money you can from your father's estate. You should be a very rich man. Go live somewhere for your own pleasure. Don't take even one look at the possibilities of power that will be presented to you. It corrupts. I was a decent and happy man until the temptation got too great. Run away from it, Johnny."

"You sonofabitch," Johnny said in a monotone. "You killed my father. Your hired man killed my girl. You sonofabitch."

Clarke managed to get up out of his chair. "Shall we go to wherever it is we're going?" he asked Kramer.

Johnny watched them go, and then he stood up. "I have to go to the office," he said in a bitter voice. "Advice or no advice."

Olin turned away from the window. He watched Johnny go, and then he looked at me. "You're wondering if I would have shot her," he said. He smiled. "It was my strictly legal night, Haskell. Lieutenant Hardy wouldn't let me have any bullets in my gun."

Mr. Gamayel was all smiles. "I don't know how to thank you, Mr. Chambrun. The return of my documents and knowing that they have always been in safe hands is the difference to me between life and death."

Chambrun looked at me. "Would you believe that all the time Mr. Gamayel's documents were locked in my office safe?"

"I don't believe anything I've seen or heard so far," I said, and headed for the Jack Daniels bottle on the sideboard.

IT WAS SEVERAL DRINKS LATER—as a matter of fact the first gray light of morning was showing at the windows—when Chambrun began to put the pieces together in some kind of order. Miss Ruysdale had set up a tape recorder on his desk.

"We're going to have to make some sort of formal statement later in the day," Chambrun said. "The tape will help remind us of anything we've left out."

It was what I might have called a family gathering except for the man with green glasses—Miss Ruysdale, Jerry Dodd, Lieutenant Hardy, Chambrun and me.

"Tortoise and the hare," Hardy said, chewing on the stem of his black pipe. He looked like a very tired man, but quite happy. "My job is slow. Check on everything. Check and keep checking. Everybody who had even a remote connection with the case rated a checking. So when Emory Clarke's room was searched by the B Plan people, I asked one of my boys to pick up some of his fingerprints. It turned out to be a ten-strike. We were able to match the thumbprint we'd found on the headboard of J. W. Sassoon's bed." Hardy looked at me. "All of a sudden we had our killer—Sassoon's killer—and you were on your way up to the penthouse for the second time. No way to stop you while we reorganized our thinking."

Chambrun put down his demi-tasse of Turkish coffee. "Clarke crumpled," he said. "Strange man, with all his talk of decency. He had it, you know. But he had gone up to the top of the mountain and he'd been tempted by what he saw. All his life he'd played a minor role in the drama of power. He'd been an adviser to the top men, but he'd never had any of it for himself. Somewhere along the way he met Valerie Brent, the alleged grief-stricken widow, who was panting for revenge against Sassoon. I imagine it took a while for them to get down to brass tacks, but I think Clarke persuaded her that the best revenge would be to hit J. W. Sassoon in his power structure, to coin a phrase. She changed her attitude toward Sassoon, which pleased his vanity. Our friend Olin, here, never believed in that change, but he couldn't convince the old man.''

"But I kept on watching her," Olin said. "I told you the truth about those clothes she bought. They were never stolen from her." He smiled. "But now we have a picture of amateurs at work."

"Gamayel's deal was the way Clarke saw to break J.W. and get power for himself," Chambrun said. "He and Valerie now had professional help. Valerie had introduced Clarke to Treadway. Clarke was shocked when he learned the truth about Valerie Brent, but he was too far committed to turn back."

"What truth?" I asked.

"Treadway was Valerie's lover," Chambrun said. "Had been for more than five years."

"Jesus!" I said. "Clarke told you that?"

"He told us," Chambrun said. "And you had just about reached the penthouse by then. No way to tell you that Valerie was in no danger at all. You were the hostage Treadway would use against us."

"The reason Treadway was here five years ago, and then two years ago," Hardy said, "wasn't professional. He was here to be with the woman he loved. I'm guessing now, but I think we'll get to prove it. Michael Brent hadn't found something out about Sassoon, as Mrs. Brent told us. He'd found out about her and Treadway. In his Middle East research he had come up with stuff on Treadway. He threatened to use it. So Valerie and her lover killed him. Her grief and her passion for revenge were total phonies."

I guess I was in shock. She had seemed so lovely, so in need of help.

"Olin mentioned amateurs," Chambrun said. "Night before last Clarke had a summons from J.W. The old man wanted advice on the papers Gamayel had brought him. When Clarke heard what was in those papers, he knew that if he could get them he would be in the driver's seat. Somehow he gave himself away. The old man accused him. He tried to call for help, and Clarke grappled with him to keep J.W. from getting to the bedside phone. The old man was screaming and Clarke tried to silence him with a pillow. The old man died under his hands. Clarke made a quick, frantic search of the room, but he couldn't find the documents. He panicked. He went to find Valerie and Treadway. He found her and told her what had happened. They couldn't locate Treadway. He'd gone out of the hotel somewhere. Clarke was afraid someone—Olin perhaps—would know he'd had an appointment with J.W. They had to make it look like something else." Chambrun's mouth moved in a bitter smile. "The lady thought of sex. Sex had always gotten her everything she wanted. They went back to J.W.'s apartment, and she took her newly bought lingerie—bought to make Treadway happy—with her. Clarke went through the difficult business of undressing J.W. and leaving him naked on the bed. Valerie spread her lingerie around. They made another quick search for the documents and, failing to find them, left."

"Amateurs always blow it," Olin said. "Chambrun determined at once that the lingerie had never been worn and any half-wit cop could have traced their purchaser through the labels."

"Our talents are small, but we plug along," Hardy said.

"And about the time we'd figured that far," Chambrun said, "we had a call from you saying Treadway was coming out via the mezzanine and the fire stairs."

"You've left out something," I said. "The kidnapping."

"Perhaps that does come next," Chambrun said. "You see, there was no kidnapping."

I gave him a blank stare. "Come again," I said.

"You'll have to rewrite your estimate of Johnny Sassoon," Chambrun said. "He may have been an idiot about hotel management, but he isn't without courage and J.W. trusted him. Sequence of events: after Olin had looked at the papers and taken off for Washington—"

"The old man had to know where the State Department would stand if a coup took place in Gamayel's country," Olin said.

"The old man was nervous about keeping those papers in his room until Olin got back from Washington. He called Johnny. Johnny came to the room and the old man gave him the documents to put in my safe—Johnny's safe at that point in time. It was after the papers were safely gone that the old man sent for Clarke."

"You said there was no kidnapping?"

"When J.W. was found dead, Johnny guessed that someone had been after the documents. He might very well be the next target. After he'd gone to the offices of J. W. Sassoon Enterprises, he left to come back to the hotel. But he didn't, of course. He went to a flea-bag place somewhere and holed in. He called Carlson and pretended to be a kidnapper. Then he made a fatal mistake. He called his room here at the Beaumont and got Trudy Woodson, who was waiting there for him. He told her he was faking the kidnapping, that she'd be named to bring him the ransom money, that they'd take off together. He told her the only thing they could do was to get away. 'Because,' he said to her, 'you know and I know who killed my father.' It seems they suspected Treadway without knowing for whom Treadway was working. He was an enemy hatchet man."

"Treadway picked up that conversation on the listening device," Hardy said. "Treadway got to Trudy and that was one of them out of the way. Johnny didn't know this had happened until you, Mark, went to that phone booth in her place."

"Treadway wore that disguise Jerry found when he went to Trudy's room to kill her?" I asked.

"He couldn't risk being seen—as Treadway—going to her room or leaving it," Chambrun said. "Now Johnny went into action. As I've said, he wasn't a genius at running a hotel, but there were people who liked him—and there were people who felt they owed him, as the new manager, loyalty. Johnny came out of his hiding place and managed to get into the basement area of the hotel. He waited until his loyal staff member showed up and he got the whole story from him of what was going on. This staff member had just seen Mark take Mr. Gamayel to his apartment and leave him there. Johnny got to a coin box phone and called Mark's rooms. He told Gamayel he knew where the documents were. And he did! They were in my safe. I haven't had occasion all day to open that safe. He persuaded Gamayel to come to where he was in the basement. The best way Johnny could get even with his enemies was to make a deal with Gamayel. He had to be sure Gamayel would play along with him, now that J.W. was dead. While he and Gamayel were discussing this, the staff member came and told him someone had bombed the apartment. Johnny and Gamayel made a quick decision. They would come to me, in the open, and get me to open the safe and turn over the documents to them. They walked in here just as you were starting down from the penthouse." Chambrun leaned back in his chair. "We had to do some quick thinking, Mark. You were the one in danger, not Mrs. Brent." He glanced at Olin. The green glasses hid all expression on that one's face. "The true professional came up with the answer. He, Treadway's enemy, would make the threat. Treadway would be certain that none of us would shoot Mrs. Brent in cold blood, but Olin was something else again. Olin was capable of doing what he threatened to do. Treadway would almost certainly push Mrs. Brent out of danger and try to get Olin."

"It took some courage," Hardy said, fumbling with his pipe, "since I wouldn't let him have a loaded gun. I wasn't sure he wouldn't go through with it if he had the chance."

"We were, literally, only seconds ahead of you in getting into place," Chambrun said. "We got the driver out of the car and replaced him with a cop. I hadn't even been able to take cover when the door opened and you appeared, with the woman and Treadway behind you." He took a cigarette out of his silver case and lit it, his eyes narrowed against the smoke. "And that," he said, "is that."

Return to the scene of the crime with Worldwide Mysteries!

REMEMBER TO KILL ME—Hugh Pentecost $3.50   ☐
Pierre Chambrun, manager of the Hotel Beaumont in New York,
must cope with the shooting of a close friend, a hostage situation
and a gang of hoods terrorizing guests.

DEADLY INNOCENTS—Mark Sadler $3.50   ☐
A brutal murder leads private investigator Paul Shaw to a man
who will pay quite handsomely if Shaw will forget the case and
go home. But for Shaw, murder is a living....

SCENT OF DEATH—Emma Page $3.50   ☐
A standard missing persons case soon mushrooms into a
horrifying double homicide when Detectives Lambert and Kelsey
find two young women in an abandoned shed, strangled.
Not available in Canada

CHAOS OF CRIME—Dell Shannon $3.50   ☐
Amid a panorama of fear and evil, Luis Mendoza of the LAPD is
up against one of his grisliest cases ever when he searches for a
psychotic sex killer who is prowling the city.

Total Amount	$ _____
Plus 75¢ Postage	.75
Payment enclosed	$ _____

Please send a check or money order payable to Worldwide Mysteries.

In the U.S.A.

Worldwide Mysteries
901 Fuhrmann Blvd.
Box 1325
Buffalo, NY 14269-1325

In Canada

Worldwide Mysteries
P.O. Box 609
Fort Erie, Ontario
L2A 5X3

Please Print

Name: _____

Address: _____

City: _____

State/Prov: _____

Zip/Postal Code: _____

WORLDWIDE LIBRARY

MYS-4

Worldwide Mysteries are keeping America in suspense with spine-tingling tales by award-winning authors.

Winner of the Grand Master Award from the Mystery Writers of America, Dorothy Salisbury Davis "...has few equals in setting up a puzzle, complete with misdirection and surprises."

DOROTHY SALISBURY DAVIS
LULLABY OF MURDER

A Julie Hayes Mystery

When the infamous New York gossip columnist, Tony Alexander, is found murdered, reporter Julie Hayes starts digging and discovers a lot of people are happier with Tony dead! As murder takes center stage, Julie finds herself caught in a web of hate, deceit and revenge, dirty deals and small-town scandals.

Can you keep a secret?

You can keep this one plus 2 free novels.

FREE BOOKS/GIFT COUPON

Mail to: The Mystery Library
901 Fuhrmann Blvd.
P.O. Box 1867
Buffalo, N.Y. 14269-1867

YES! Please send me 2 free books from the Mystery Library and my free surprise gift. Then send me 2 mystery books, first time in paperback, every month. Bill me only $3.50 per book. There is *no* extra charge for shipping and handling! There is no minimum number of books I must purchase. I can always return a shipment and cancel at any time. Even if I never buy another book from The Mystery Library, the 2 free books and the surprise gift are mine to keep forever.

414 BPY BPS9

Name	(PLEASE PRINT)	
Address		Apt. No.
City	State	Zip

This offer is limited to one order per household and not valid to present subscribers. Terms and prices subject to change without notice.

MYS-BPA6